Homecoming Queen and Other Twisted Tales

Homecoming Queen and Other Twisted Tales

Michele Sheldon

Beastling Publishing

I'd like to thank all the people who have encouraged me to keep writing short stories over the years and have come along to our Hand of Doom story nights, especially my sister Sara and my partner Graham and our children Laurie, Samuel and Luke who were often dragged along to story readings without much choice and always bore them stoically.

CONTENTS

CONTENTS

Call Me Mr Moogle

It started as a tiny lump on the inside of my bottom lip.

I used to flick my tongue over it every now and then, telling myself that if it grew, I should probably visit the doctor. Two weeks later, I woke one morning to find it had erupted through my skin. It felt like a separate entity, a slimy island.

I went to the bathroom and pulled down my lower lip and a swollen pink bump stared back. It was about the size and shape of a tooth; a spare but useless molar I could almost pop into a gap left by a tooth long gone.

I went straight to the doctor.

An emergency, I said.

Nothing to worry about, she said. It will go over the next few days; just one of those things. Keep an eye on it and if it changes shape or gets any bigger, come back immediately.

She didn't say anything about it starting to talk.

I was in the kitchen doing the washing up when it first spoke. I was listening to a play on the radio about a kids' home and I kept hearing squeaking, thinking perhaps it was part of the play's sound effects, some children messing around, or perhaps a seagull on a rooftop squawking about something or other.

But then I heard a clear, Hello! Hello! It was if someone was out in the street trying to attract the attention of an acquaintance, unsure whether the person would turn around, let alone recognise them.

Over here! the high-pitched voice said.

I didn't want to listen to strangers' inane conversations, so I turned the radio up.

But when I went to bed a few hours later and pulled back my bottom lip to check on my lump, I heard that same voice again.

Hello! Hello! Over here! it squeaked.

I peered out of the window into the dark street below. It was deserted apart from next door's over-fluffed black cat ambling along the pavement.

I went back to the mirror and pulled down my lip once more.

I'm here, you big fat idiot! it said.

I noticed then how the words were being formed by a miniscule red gash of a mouth in the middle of the lump, its upper lip sporting a fine downy auburn moustache and two misshapen teeth. And, when I saw its network of tiny veins pulsating like a heart, I screamed.

You ain't so pretty yourself! it said with a spitefulness I quickly came to dread.

* * *

It made me call him Mr Moogle. If I didn't refer to him by his correct title, he'd bite me and I'd feel a sharp pain, followed by the metallic tang of my own blood. And once his moustache grew long, he used his teeth to pull at the thick hair hanging over his mouth, making me shriek.

Then I had to say, Okay, Mr Moogle, I'll do it.

I had to be extra cautious when he started growing his tiny blue fish eye. Even though his eyesight was rubbish, if I yawned or spoke to someone then he'd snatch a glimpse of the outside world which usually meant trouble.

Once we walked past a poster in the Post Office advertising the Russian State Circus. Mr Moogle must have seen a flash of the exotic lady standing on top of a too-white pony as I yawned. The circus had set up in the park near to the train station and, even though we'd walked past on various Mr Moogle missions, he'd been oblivious to all the caravans pulling up, the big top being erected and the shabbily-dressed clowns blocking pavements and thrusting discount flyers into the faces of passers-by.

Mr Moogle wants to go to the circus, he said, scraping his teeth against the inside of my mouth.

That afternoon I bought a cheap back row ticket for the matinee performance.

The circus had a Rasputin theme running through it. All the performers had fixed grins on their over-made up faces but you could tell they'd much rather kill you. And who could blame them? That annoying Boney M record *Ra-Ra-Rasputin* played between the acts. Mr Moogle insisted on singing along, and a boy and his mother, sitting in front of us, kept turning and giving me funny looks.

Quieten down, I told Mr Moogle.

But he bit me and I couldn't help cry out.

During the interval, the boy and his mum moved to the expensive empty seats at the front but were frogmarched back to their former seats by the bouncer, who then gestured for me to leave.

Mr Moogle came out with a mouthful of bad words as the bouncer held open the canvas flap and shoved me into the daylight.

Thanks for nothing, said Mr Moogle, before biting into my cheek.

As he and his fish eye grew, he liked to read the newspaper in the mornings over breakfast, not allowing me turn the page until he'd finished. That's where he saw the advert for the *Smurfs'* movie, a month after his arrival. He made me push my lip right into Papa Smurf's smile so that my head was buried in his newspaper print beard and I began to dribble.

There are some things you cannot make me do, I said, after he'd permitted me to move.

Two hours later, we were queuing in the rain for the 12pm showing.

* * *

His Build a Bear 'birthday party' was the final straw.

But you've only been here for five weeks, I said. How can it be your birthday?

Mr Moogle wants a birthday party. Mr Moogle gets a birthday party. I want a koala, and Mrs Moogle wants a panda.

There is no Mrs Moogle, I said through gritted teeth.

I wasn't going to admit that I'd felt another little lump erupting in the far corner of my mouth that morning, and quickly took out a soft white tissue from my pocket as the familiar taste of blood filled my mouth.

After I'd stuffed the bears with beige fluff, he made me browse the shop, with my bottom lip pulled down so he could view all the bear-shaped outfits available; sailors, ballet dancers, beachwear, cowboys, Star Wars, Batman, pirate wear, even a sinister-looking Iron Man costume complete with mask. Everything was £10 or over except for a pair of fat bear trainers for a fiver. I was out of work at the time and didn't have the kind of money to throw away on outfits for toys and Mr Moogle knew it. But round and round we went, four, five, six times with him yelling at me to stop spinning the displays so quickly. When I glanced up, the shop assistants, previously helpful, had lost their friendly smiles and were whispering behind the cover of their hands.

Out of earshot in the wig section, I told Mr Moogle that everything was too expensive; the panda and koala would have to remain naked for now.

But Mr Moogle wants a pretty outfit for Mrs Moogle's panda, he said, pulling at a few strands of his moustache with his teeth. I winced. My mouth was full of unhealed Mr Moogle bites. I couldn't bear any more.

I took the blonde wig, silver bikini and red pair of kitten mules up to the counter and paid with my credit card.

* * *

When I got home I went straight to the kitchen, took my sharpest vegetable knife from the drawer, walked to the bathroom mirror and grabbed Mr Moogle's moustache. He came off nice and clean, and I left him screaming in the sink next to my morning's toothpaste spit.

I bled all over the bathroom, down the stairs, in my car and over the A&E waiting room and several nurses. After stitching me up, the doctors kept me in overnight, referring me for psychiatric reports.

That was fine with me. I was in no hurry to return home. I relaxed, relishing the thought of Mr Moogle dying a slow death without my blood to feed him; a dried up Mr Moogle, a lump of hairy gristle with a shrunken eye. I decided that as soon as I was discharged, I'd scoop up his body in some old Tupperware, take it to the doctors and ask, do you believe me now?

But when I returned home two days later, there was nothing there; just a toothpaste stain dyed red with my blood.

Sometimes, I wonder if a spider dragged him away to its lair to feast on him. But then when it's really quiet, just before dawn, when the seagulls are still dreaming, I think I can hear him berating me about something I haven't done to his satisfaction. And it makes me wonder if he's just biding his time before he comes and finds me and the lovely Mrs Moogle.

First published Black Pear's Day of the Dead anthology and Storgy.

Great-Uncle Randolph

'What do you mean by a few odd beliefs?' I ask.

We're already two hours into the journey to visit my boy-friend's great-uncle Randolph and it's only just occurred to Paul to tell me.

'Nothing really...just a load of mumbo jumbo,' he says, squinting into the glow of the low winter sun. 'I thought I'd better mention it in case you get a bit of a shock.'

'A shock? What do you mean?'

'Randolph's a bit of a character, that's all.'

'In my book that usually means he has offensive views,' I say, glancing behind me as I hear Jack stirring in his car seat. 'He's not a racist or a pervert, is he?'

'No, of course not. He's only offensive if you're religious.'

'What kind of religious?'

'Well, of a mainstream faith.'

'Well, he's hardly going to offend me then, is he...unless he's a druid? I hate druids. All that running around stone circles business.'

'Nothing so colourful, I'm afraid.'

'A devil worshipper then? Rosemary's Baby. You've made a pact with the devil for Jack,' I say, dramatically.

'No! Of course not. What a horrible idea,' says Paul, grimacing.

He glances in the mirror at Jack, who has just started babbling to himself as if he's alarmed at the thought too.

'What then?'

'He just waffles on about reincarnation sometimes, that's all.'

'Paul, I know I haven't slept for the last few months but I think I can handle a bit of Buddhism.'

'Just thought I'd better warn you,' Paul smiles.

'He can waffle on all he likes after giving us all that money...'

I was about to add *although it was a shame we had to stay for the whole weekend* but I kept it to myself to avoid an argument. Paul thought me overly anxious and protective of Jack. When the invite arrived the day after the cash appeared in our joint account, I felt we couldn't refuse.

Paul begins indicating for the next junction off the motorway and we head into the Kent countryside, the sun moving behind us. Now I can see properly, I'm struck how tired the countryside looks in winter, like an over-washed favourite t-shirt. It's stripped bare, standing naked in the cold November afternoon, clinging onto patches of fog as if trying to preserve some modesty. We whizz past a barbed wire fence covered in bits of black plastic and I scan the field for a herd of bin bag animals racing through.

We're barely off the motorway when we come to a tiny village, lined with well-preserved timber-framed houses, and follow the narrow road into the village square. A few cars are parked outside a pub. Its chimney puffs out a steady plume of smoke as do a few regulars standing outside, who glance in our direction before resuming their conversation. Paul pulls over, opposite a pair of imposing iron gates. On either side are stone pillars adorned by carved pineapples. Beyond the gates lies a long gravel driveway at the end of which stands a Jacobean mansion. It's surrounded by terraced gardens, sweeping down to a lake fringed by woods.

Paul undoes his seat belt and climbs out of the car.

'We can't just park here,' I say to his back.

Paul ignores me and presses a buzzer on the inside of the pillar and I suddenly get it.

I wind down the window.

'Bloody hell, Paul. You could have warned me. I didn't bring anything fancy to wear.'

I knew Paul's family were all minor aristocrats. Barons and baronesses who own a handful of crumbling mansions between them. You know the type. Worth millions on paper and always pleading poverty, though somehow they always manage to afford private schools and expensive holidays.

However, Paul had told me his uncle had made a fortune in the dot com boom. Subsequently, he'd managed to buy back the house that'd been the family seat for 350 years after the previous owner, a Seventies rock star, had died in a car crash.

Paul climbs back into the car and looks at me then, all wide blue eyes.

'It's not like Downton Abbey, you know. He doesn't expect guests to get dressed for dinner.'

'He wants us naked?'

'Ha, ha.'

'Still. It's intimidating,' I say. 'It's bigger than the village I grew up in and look at all those disgusting crows.'

I nod my head towards the house. Dozens of them are sitting on its turrets. As we drive through the gates, they take off as one. It sounds like a giant straightening out a wet sheet before hanging it out to dry on a washing line. A few white spots hit the car windscreen as the crows fly overhead. I watch them settle on a skeleton tree, repopulating its leaves with their wings. They call to one another, perhaps complaining about us visitors disturbing them, or had they spotted Jack in the car? Growing up on a farm I'd witnessed the way a murder of crows would live up to its name: ganging up on a new-born lamb and pecking out its eyes for sport.

I look behind me as Jack begins fussing, making the 'eh, eh, eh' noises I so dread in the middle of the night.

'He's building for a cry,' I say checking my phone. 'It's been three hours since the last feed. He'll be hungry. You go in and I'll stay in the car and feed him.'

Paul gives me his arched eyebrows look that says I'm the one that's fussing.

'Bring him inside. It'll be nice and warm.'

'It's easier on our own,' I say getting out of the car and opening the back door.

'Really?'

'Yes, really. Go on, go.'

Paul takes the bags from the boot and half waves as he walks up the steps to the front door. When I look up a moment later, he's gone.

I'm pleased to have some time to myself with Jack. I'd only just settled into breastfeeding again after having a painful bout of mastitis. It was other people too. It was stressful enough trying to get a baby to latch on without having to breathe in other people's disapproval. Paul's parents had only visited twice but each time I'd fed Jack, Paul's father had turned puce and I'd had to hide in the bedroom, while his mother came and sat next to me, suggesting I get Jack on the bottle as soon as possible.

Twenty minutes later Jack's appetite is sated and he's fast asleep. I place him gently back in the car seat, glare at the crows stationed back on their turrets and carry him up the stone steps to the house, feeling the chill of the departing sun biting into my bones.

The door has been left on the latch. I shove it hard with my shoulder. It creaks loudly as if complaining about the force I've used and I cringe, praying it won't wake Jack.

I blink in the darkness until I can see in the dim light. The hall is quilted in dark wooden panels and dozens of extravagantly decorated gold-framed portraits. Many show handsome dark-haired, blue-eyed men riding equally handsome horses, hunting or dressed for battle. The family resemblance is so uncanny that I stop in my tracks as I see Paul smiling down at me, dressed as an Edwardian gent with bushy sideburns. The portrait looks like it's half finished, the rest of the details hidden away as if they've only appeared for my benefit. I look away and then back again to test my theory and see that man has a smaller mouth than Paul and a pudgier face.

I walk on, listening for sounds of life, and come to a row of portraits of women, all with dark-haired tresses piled upon their heads, the same striking blue eyes as the men, all watching my progress. I feel a quickening of my heart as I remember the first time I met Paul's mum and dad, how delighted they seemed that we looked so similar. Like brother and sister, they'd commented, glancing at one another.

'Bella?'

I turn to see Paul.

'Jesus, you scared me,' I say, my heart thumping.

'We're ready for you now,' he says in a silly monster voice before taking the car seat from me.

'What have you been feeding him? He weighs a tonne!' he says walking off down the corridor.

I follow, past more portraits, into a huge sitting room with a large window and doors leading out onto the terraced garden and the lake beyond.

At first, I think the room is empty and I stare out at the view, watching the sun dipping behind the tops of the trees, bathing the grounds in an eerie orange glow. A crow waddles past with a small twig in its mouth.

'Uncle Randolph? They're here!'

I look round and see a man squatting. He's stirring the fire with a long metal poker and is dwarfed by the size of the stone mantelpiece which stretches across a third of the room.

'Jack and Bella!' he says, turning to look at us, his eyes searching out the sleeping bundle in the car seat.

He gets up and I'm surprised how fit he looks despite his age and illness; slim and straight-backed. He's dressed in a black polo neck jumper and red corduroy trousers, putting me in mind of a

1960s knitting pattern model. As he gets closer I see he has the same dark blue eyes as Paul, flecked with gold.

He takes the car seat from Paul and places Jack on an armchair next to the fire.

'Gets a bit draughty as the sun goes down,' he says.

He bends down, peering in at a sleeping Jack.

I keep glancing at Jack and the fire, mentally calculating the distance a spark could fly.

'Lovely looking boy,' he says to Paul. 'Blue eyes, I assume.'

'Most Caucasian babies are born with blue eyes,' I say, moving to stand between Jack and the fire.

'Though Jack's are unusually light, almost violet,' says Paul.

'Well done you. Just the ticket,' says Randolph, bending and stroking Jack's cheek.

Randolph must have read my mind because he straightens up and walks over to the fireplace towards a large ornate fireguard.

'I'll do that,' says Paul.

He manoeuvres the guard around the fire while Randolph comes over and gives me a kiss on each cheek.

'Well done you too Bella and lovely to meet you. Paul has told me so much about you.'

I smile, wondering exactly what Paul has told him. That we'd only been together for three weeks when I got pregnant? That he'd dumped his long-term girlfriend for me? That I'd only just qualified as a teacher and hadn't planned to have children in my early twenties? That he'd promised to look after me and the baby, whether or not our relationship worked out?

'Thank you so much for the money. It's...,' I begin to say.

But he's holding up a hand.

'It's the least I could do. I haven't been blessed with children. You and Paul are incredibly fortunate to have such a lovely baby boy. And I can't take it with me. Paul told you, I assume?'

'Yes, I'm so sorry. Is there nothing that the doctors can do?'

'They could blast me with chemo and give me another couple of months but I'd rather not. I'm 78. I've had a good innings.'

'I'm so sorry,' I say glancing across at Paul, who is bending down and stroking Jack's tiny hand.

'No, no. Please. That's what's so ridiculous about the illness. I feel fine at the moment. Tomorrow may be a different matter; I won't be able to get out of bed. But you're not here to talk about me. We're here to celebrate the birth of your beautiful son.'

We sit and drink tea and I pile up far too much cream and jam on my scones, listening to the fire crackling while Paul and Randolph catch up on family gossip. I try and keep up with the conversation, asking questions every now and then. They do their best to include me, explaining who is who and why something is funny. I understand. My three sisters and brother do the same. It can be annoying having to explain every relationship, sharing family jokes that others don't find funny, especially when time is so precious for Randolph, who'd been given just three months to live.

So I eventually leave them to it and zone out, the warmth of the fire lulling me to sleep.

* * *

When I wake, my head feels muddled and I have to resist the urge to fall back to sleep. The room is in semi-darkness and I feel a panic rising, wondering where I am. I glance around the room, screwing my eyes up at the dying embers.

I look at the car seat next to me, noting the straps are undone and the absence of chubby little legs.

'Jack!'

My fingers probe the car seat as if Jack is hiding beneath its padding. The material is still warm to touch, and I feel a sudden longing to nuzzle into Jack's soft skin and smell his milky scent.

'Paul?' I say, though I know the room is empty.

It's the first time I've been separated from Jack, I realise, and it feels like I'm missing a limb. It's also the first time I've slept through Jack waking. And another thought comes: perhaps he didn't wake. Perhaps Paul or even Randolph picked him up and woke him.

I pick up the car seat and manage to navigate my way to the door by the last of the dim firelight and into the corridor. It's like stepping into a winter's day. A cold draught follows me as I feel my way along the wooden panelling, my teeth involuntarily chattering.

I want to shout for Paul but I feel foolish for being so afraid and soon enough I'm greeted with the faint smell of roast chicken. My stomach growls as I sniff my way along the corridor and turn into another, past several closed doors. I berate myself for being silly. Paul had promised to cook Sunday lunch. Jack must have dirtied his nappy. Paul had changed him and kept him with him while I slept. *They wanted me to sleep, idiot*, I think to myself. *They're being kind*. The smell of roast chicken is so strong now that I know I'm close and, at the end of the corridor, I find myself at the entrance to a surprisingly small kitchen.

I'm about to go in but stop as I see Paul holding an elongated Jack at arm's length. My eyes widen as I take in the long frilly white gown sweeping to the floor. Behind them, I catch sight of Randolph sharpening a carving knife.

'What's going on?'

Paul turns and smiles a little too brightly. It's the same look he gave me when I caught him talking to his ex-girlfriend on the phone last week.

'You're awake. We thought we'd let you sleep. He did a bit of stinker, I'm afraid,' he says.

Randolph stands next to Paul and Jack. The knife in his hand glints in the row of ceiling lights shining directly above him. They're so bright they blanch all colour from Randolph's cheeks, making him appear like a husk of himself.

I have an urge to grab the knife from him and throw it far away.

'Paul said you didn't care for red meat? Roast chicken all right?' asks Randolph.

'Why's Jack dressed like that?'

'Oh, it's the family christening gown. I hope you don't mind? It's a bit of a family tradition,' says Randolph.

Jack is squirming in Paul's hands and holds his little arms out to me. I take him from Paul, wanting to rip the horrible garment off. It smells musty and old and is stiff with starch.

Jack begins to grizzle. I jig him gently in my arms.

'I don't think it can be very comfortable for him,' I say, holding Jack out for Paul to take. 'You hold him and I'll take it off.'

'He was fine before you came in. He must have smelt the milk,' says Paul, taking Jack.

I shoot him a dark look. He knows how much I hate feeling like a cow, always having to be ready to feed, whether or not I was asleep or in pain.

'But he looks so sweet in it,' says Randolph, still holding the knife as he bends down so his face is practically touching Jack's. 'Don't you, my little angel.'

'I wouldn't like to get any food on it,' I say to Randolph, 'or *milk*,' I say to Paul.

'It's no problem,' says Randolph.

He stumbles as he straightens up. I put my arm out to steady him and take the knife.

'The gown has been in the family for 200 years. I dare say it's seen its fair share of regurgitated milk and other bodily fluids,' says Randolph, brushing me off. 'I can manage, thank you.'

I place the knife in the sink and take back Jack, settling him in the car seat.

Paul hovers over me.

'You go and make yourself comfortable,' says Paul, picking up the car seat and placing it on sideboard. 'We'll bring Jack in a minute.'

'No, it's okay, I'll take him with me,' I say.

Paul lowers his voice to a whisper and places his hand on my shoulder.

'Come on, Bella. Randolph really hasn't got long.'

* * *

Highly polished silverware, laid out neatly on the table, winks at me as I walk into the dining room. Large cabinets line the far wall, showcasing a hotchpotch of ornaments: miniature elephants sculpted from their own tusks, silver giraffes and lions hiding behind colourful glass bowls and jugs, little silver penguin salt and pepper pots, all covered in a fine layer of dust. I sit and gape at the display of wealth. Everything in the cabinet is probably worth more than my father had ever earned into his entire life as a farm labourer. I turn my attention back to the table and lift the lids off the various dishes; roast potatoes, sprouts, carrots and peas, my tummy rumbling loudly, despite the recent scoffing of scones.

A few minutes later, Randolph appears at the door carrying the chicken on a sliver tray, followed by Paul carrying Jack in the car seat. Randolph places the chicken at the head of the table, while Paul puts Jack on the floor next to me, the ridiculous white gown billowing out around him like a wedding dress.

'We took Jack on a tour of the house while you slept,' says Randolph. 'Show Bella the photos while I carve,' he adds.

A frown slithers over Paul's forehead as he takes his phone from his pocket.

'I'm sorry. I didn't mean to fall asleep like that...' I say.

'No problem, Bella. You must be exhausted. Anyway, I defy anyone not to fall asleep in Lympne Manor. It lulls you to sleep. It's well known for it,' says Randolph.

Paul hurriedly scrolls through the photos. They're almost all of Randolph holding Jack, gazing down at him admiringly with a few selfies of Paul and Randolph beaming into the camera with poor Jack squashed between them.

'We took him to see the chapel,' says Randolph, carving through the golden skin into the creamy white flesh.

A photo flashes up of Jack in Randoph's arms standing by a large marble font.

'We thought we'd show him where all his ancestors were christened.'

'You don't still use it?' I say, trying to increase the size of the image as I catch sight of something glistening on Jack's forehead.

'I hope that's not what I think it is?'

'No, it's just a smear, some gravy or something on the screen,' Paul grins, wiping it away with his sleeve. 'You think me and Randolph sneaked off to get Jack christened without you?'

'No, of course not,' I say, smiling across at Randolph.

'Anyway, I think Randolph needs help,' says Paul, trying to take the phone. But in doing so, another image flashes by with a fourth person in the picture.

'Hang on, Paul,' I say, snatching the phone and scrolling back until I find it.

As I look closer, I can see it's of Randolph holding baby Jack up to a huge portrait of a heavily bearded man, who has the same piercing dark blue eyes of Paul's family.

Paul leans across and tries to reclaim his phone again.

'No wait.'

I stare at the photo, unable to tear my eyes away.

'He looks so real … it's like he's photo-bombing.'

But there's something else. Something I daren't say: it looks as if Randolph is holding Jack up like an offering.

'That's my father,' says Randolph, glancing across at the image on the phone. 'I'm afraid he'll be looming down on you all night.'

I look at Paul, puzzled.

'His portrait is in the room where we're staying.'

'Oh...'

'He was a great magician,' says Randolph.

'You didn't tell me, Paul,' I say, realising it was a stupid question. We knew very little about each other, let alone each other's family.

'Wow! What kind of magician?'

'Illusions mostly but he also fancied himself as a bit of a Houdini.'

Paul rolls his eyes at me, like he's heard this story a million times before.

'One time he got the servants to truss him up and then dunked himself in the lake. They were all standing around waiting for him to emerge – if he didn't after five minutes they were to wade in and rescue him. Anyway, several minutes passed and the butler was about to run in when he felt a tap on his shoulder. He turned round and father was stood right behind him, having shed off the ropes and most of his clothing.'

'Did he tell you how he did it?' I ask.

'No, never. But I do know that the lake is very shallow and that there used to be a tunnel at the lake's edge which supposedly leads to the chapel.'

'Did he ever perform?'

'Oh no, not to the public. Only for friends. He and Aleister used to experiment a lot and enjoy practical jokes, mostly at other people's expense.'

'Aleister? His brother?' I ask.

'No, Aleister Crowley. He was quite famous at the time.'

'Alestier Crowley? Hang on a moment, wasn't he a devil worshipper?' I say glancing at Paul.

'Not at all! He was great man who thought most religions were absurd, especially Christianity, so how on earth could one believe in the devil? No, he had some odd beliefs but he was a true friend,' he says, gazing at the picture.

'...to your father,' corrects Paul.

'Sorry?'

'To your father. Not to you,' says Paul, speaking a little louder, glancing at me nervously and then back at Randolph.

'Yes, sorry, to father,' he says before passing around the plates of chicken.

'He got a terrible press. But he believed in the divine spirit and how we can live forever.'

'Live forever?'

'Yes, he developed a method of regenerating his spirit into the living.'

'What like Dr Who?'

'Fictional character. But yes, if you like.'

'And you believed him?' I ask.

'Please help yourself to vegetables,' says Randolph.

I feel Paul searching for my hand under the table and squeezing it. We eat in silence, save for the scraping of forks and knives on plates, and throughout, I fret that I've offended a dying man. When I finish, I glance at Randolph. He looks at me then as if he's surprised to see me sitting in his dining room.

'Why don't we take Bella to the chapel in the woods tomorrow?' says Paul in the silence.

'Bella to the woods?' he says, scrunching his eyes shut.

'Yes, show her the chapel where we took Jack today?'

He opens his eyes then and stares wildly at me.

'Yes, sorry. Lapses. I have these lapses all the time. It's the medication. Apologies Bella.'

Jack opens his eyes too. And as if suddenly aware of wearing the vile gown for the first time, starts crying.

'I've set up the travel cot,' says Paul, standing and picking up the car seat. 'I'll settle them and then clear up, Randolph. Please don't touch a thing.'

'Time for bed then,' I say, getting up quickly, thankful for Jack's timely outburst. 'Good night, Randolph, and thank you.'

'No thank you, Bella,' says Randolph, wobbling slightly as he stands. 'It was so lovely to meet you. Thank you so much for bringing Jack into the world. He really is just the ticket.'

* * *

After I feed Jack in bed and settle him in the cot, I turn my back to the nursing chair and the portrait looming over it. Even so, I can still feel Paul's granddad's eyes burning into me. In fact, the portrait is so overbearing I find myself huddling under the duvet, praying that Paul will come to bed soon. But I must have fallen asleep because the next thing I hear is Jack making his 'eh, eh, eh' noises. I groan and turn the bedside light on, surprised to see Paul lying next to me.

I get out of bed and pick up Jack, ready to feed him in bed. But as soon as I try to get back in, Paul spreads his legs over my side.

'Paul,' I say. 'Move over.'

He snores his reply. I keep my eyes lowered away from the portrait and glance across at the nursing chair, inviting me to sit.

'Paul,' I try again.

'Mmmm,' he murmurs.

I want to prod him awake but Jack is properly crying now and I don't want to risk waking Randolph from his precious sleep. I hurry over and sit in the chair, trying to block out any thoughts of the portrait behind me.

I sink down and open my nightdress. Jack opens his mouth and latches on, at first suckling furiously then relaxing into a regular rhythm as my milk comes through. I let myself relax too. The chair is incredibly soft and could have been built especially for me and, before I know it, I begin to drift off but jolt awake as a cold breeze blows over me. Jack is still suckling and the curtains billow towards me like rubbish ghosts. Paul must have opened the window when he came to bed. I'm about to go and close it when I feel an icy hand on my shoulder. And, as I slowly turn to look round, I realise then that they set it up from the start. The bedroom. The position of the old nursing chair. The creepy lifelike portrait of Randolph's father looming down at us. But I suspect it went further back than arranging the furniture on the day, probably back to when I'd first met Paul at the party.

Randolph died that night. At the same time as I was feeding Jack. People wouldn't believe me if I told them. So as a rule, I don't. In fact, I never have. You're the first and I bet you won't believe me. But here goes. One minute I'm looking down to see Jack smiling at me, milk dribbling from the corner of his mouth, the next a hazy, dusty human shape walks right out of that portrait and pours itself into my beautiful baby. And when I look back down, there's no mistaking Randolph's dark blue eyes flecked with gold peering right up at me.

First published Rosebud, US literary magazine.

Green Bins, Red Tops

'I was working in my office at the time,' I said as the young policeman followed me from the hallway into the sitting room.

I felt myself blush as I noticed how the sun, streaming through the bay window, not only illuminated all the stains on the beige carpet, but also spotlighted all the smudged kids' fingerprints over the walls.

'Your office?' he asked, stepping over a half-built Lego airplane.

'Yes, at the top of the house. You get an excellent view of the street which is why I saw what I saw. Here one moment and gone the next. Like one of those magic shows on TV,' I said, gesturing for him to sit.

'Perhaps you'd like to start from the beginning,' he said, carefully perching on the edge of the sofa as if my cushions weren't good enough for his backside.

He took his notebook and pen from his top pocket and I watched his podgy fingers trying to open the pages, imagining they'd done their fair share of wall smearing not so long ago. With pen poised, he looked at me expectantly.

'Well, I was settling back into work after making a cup of tea when I heard a commotion outside. I looked out of the window and there were four men walking along – two on either side of the pavement, shouting across the street to one another.'

'What were they shouting?'

'I don't know. They were foreign…I'd say Eastern European.'

'Polish?'

'No, I don't think so. They were too dark-skinned. Romanians or Slovakians possibly?'

The policeman rolled his eyes.

'Ages?'

'Early-20s, one was a little older, perhaps early-30s. The ringleader, I'd say. Even from the top of the house I could see he had a smoker's complexion. You know that craggy, premature ageing look that smokers get… when their pores grow bigger and bigger until their skin resembles a tea bag, all perforated?'

The policeman scratched at his dark sideburns, looking at me blankly.

'Hair colour?'

'Dark, nearly shaven to the skull.'

'Clothing?'

'Yes, they were dressed,' I smiled, hoping to get one in return. His head remained bowed over his notebook.

'…it was warm and sunny…T-shirts and jeans.'

'What colour?'

'Blue jeans…sorry, I can't remember the colours of the T-shirts.'

'Dark blue jeans?'

I shrugged.

'I know the one who disappeared was wearing stone-washed denim. That's about it. Sorry.'

'So were these men arguing?'

'Oh, no. Quite the opposite. The ringleader was doing most of the shouting and gesticulating as if telling the men which house to go to.'

'Were they delivering leaflets or selling something?'

'No, no. They were scavenging. Searching driveways and bins. I was quite worried because my neighbour's having building work done. Typically, the builder had the day off but there's a skip out the front. They came right up to her front door nosing around. I nearly knocked on the window to tell them to clear off, but then I thought, well, they're doing no harm, they're just trying to survive like the rest of us.'

'And?'

'The ringleader called to his friends, and one further up the street, and another from across the road came running. Then the ringleader helped one of them into the skip for a good old rummage.'

'Find anything?'

'Yes, they took a bedside cabinet with its door hanging off. One of those 50s ones that gets up-cycled.'

The policeman furrowed his brow and I had a flash of how he'd look in a few years' time if he carried on scowling.

'You know, sprayed a vibrant colour and sold for a fat profit.'

He nodded.

'Anyway, after they found the bathroom cabinet, the one in the skip must have spotted something because he began turfing everything onto the drive, and the other two became very animated as if they'd found something really exciting. The ring-leader then got on his mobile, walking up and down the street, like he was giving directions to someone. Well, that's when I noticed the fourth man poking around in the bin at number 30 opposite.'

'What kind of bin?'

'The green bin. Household waste.'

The policeman pulled a face, flaring his nostrils, reminding me of a grumpy pony.

'That's what I thought. I lost interest in the skip after that, watching this man with his head in the bin. It must have stank because number 30 aren't exactly the cleanest.'

'And had the rubbish been collected recently?'

'No, in two days' time. And their bins are always bursting. Sometimes they have to leave an extra bag out which attracts all the foxes and seagulls. In the morning, there's a trail of pizza crusts and chips all down the street. They seem to live on them, not that I'm nosy or anything. It's just with the office overlooking the street, you -.'

'Yes, I understand,' he interrupted.

'They don't recycle either. I've seen the man checking no-one's around before furtively shoving cardboard, tins and bottles in the green bin, even though they've got two perfectly good recycling bins. They even put their old newspapers in, well, if you can call them newspapers, the red tops like *The Sun* and *Daily Mail* mostly, you know the ones always banging on about immigrants or incompetent social workers and coppers...oops...no offence.'

'None taken,' he smiled. 'And did he find anything?'

'Well, he must have done because he kept sticking his head in as if he wasn't quite sure what he'd found. But whatever it was, he was going to get it. He was on his tip-toes and did a series of little bounces and then just dived in with his legs flailing around and then -.'

'And then?

'Well, then his legs just disappeared as if he'd been yanked inside and the lid shut with a loud slap.'

The policeman looked up properly now, the corner of his lips twitching. It didn't take a mind reader to know what he was thinking; how he couldn't wait to tell his mates back at the station about the nutty woman round the corner.

'What about his friends?' he said, swallowing back half a smile.

'Well, they were busy with the skip, I'd say cock-a-hoop at this point because they'd salvaged my neighbour's old front door. It was a 1930s one. It still had its stained glass and is probably worth quite a bit. I don't know why Vicky wanted to chuck it away, and replace it with one of those cheap PVC ones. Anyway, by this point they were loading their spoils into the back of a van that had pulled up outside. Battered old thing it was, I almost felt sorry for it as it spluttered off towards town.'

'So they didn't bother to look for their friend?'

'No, but maybe they thought he'd gone further up the road and that they'd pick him up on the way.'

'And what about the bin? What did you do?'

'Well, I just put it down to seeing things at first. I convinced myself that he must have got out when I'd glanced away or something. But it troubled me for the next couple of hours. I kept staring at the bin waiting for him to jump out, or for the bin to sprout claws and teeth and start wheeling off by itself, attacking passers-by, even worse the kids… my kids…coming out of school.'

'Beware! The killer bin!' he said in mock horror before adding: 'You didn't think to go and check?'

'Well, yes, in the end I was fretting so much, I did. I went down there and checked. I braced myself and pulled up the lid, leaping back just in case -.'

'In case it pulled you in too?' he smirked.

'Yes, I suppose I did, however stupid it sounds. I crept a bit closer and peered in. It was surprisingly empty but then I suppose they are on holiday.'

'See anything?'

'Only a huge pile of soggy tabloids at the bottom and what looked like strawberry jam. To be honest, I was pretty relieved - not to mention a little embarrassed - realising I must have just imagined the whole thing. So I flipped down the lid and -.'

'And?'

'And that's when it…burped.'

'Burped?' he said, glancing up sharply.

'Yes, officer, it was a massive burp, like an old man's burp; deep and well-practised. The stench of it knocked me sideways and it was so powerful that it forced the lid to reopen with a bang.'

The policeman sat up straight now, placing his pen and note-book into his pocket.

'You know that wasting police time is a serious offence?'

'Yes, I do. But if you don't believe me, go see for yourself.'

* * *

Friday, September 9, 4pm: Interview Room 3.

'Detective Inspector Clive Wilkins present with suspect Sarah Evans, of 45 Warren Road, Folkestone re: the disappearance of PC Ian Heddon.

'I understand PC Heddon visited your home earlier this afternoon after you reported a missing person?'

'Yes, I did. But I did warn him not to get too close -.'

First published Black Pear's Day of the Dead anthology.

The Ghost Next Door

My first ever ghosts were two goblins in flat caps. They liked to push their pickled walnut faces into mine as I lay trapped in my cot, trying to quieten my screaming with their whisky breath shushes. They were cowards though because as soon as mum appeared at the door they always faded into the wall like half-finished portraits.

The fat scissor lady was ghost number three. She wore a purple nylon dressing gown and matching fluffy mule slippers which miraculously hung onto her feet as she hovered in our sitting room, slashing at an invisible enemy in the ceiling with a pair of scissors.

Mum would ask, what you looking at Emma-Jane? And I'd say, I'm looking at nothing, Mummy. Because I'd learnt from years of screaming at the wrinkly goblins that no-one but me could see them.

Then when I was six, we moved into a new house on a huge estate and I thought hooray, I'll get away from the drunk goblins and the fat scissor lady. All was quiet on the ghost front until I went into the garden. And there was ghost number four waiting for me: a young man in stripy blue pyjamas weeping, his throat all bloody jiggedy-jaggedy flesh. I offered him a Fruit Salad chew to cheer him up. But he looked straight through me as if I was the ghost.

When Mum's friends visited, she'd say to them, you'd think she'd be cock-a-hoop now we have a nice big garden with a swing and a climbing frame. But she never wants to go out, do you Emma-Jane? Don't know she's been born.

And I'd stand there, feeling my cheeks burn, wanting to say, I'd like to see you lot try and enjoy yourself with all that sobbing in the background.

As I grew older, and my world expanded, the number of ghosts I encountered dramatically increased. Most of my friends' memories of school trips were prompted by what particular chocolate bar or packet of crisps they'd eaten; mine was whatever ghost I'd chanced upon.

Dover Castle was by far the worst, prompting me to start my ghost spotter's notebook. During the hour-long tour of the Secret Wartime Tunnels, we were followed around by a blond-haired soldier dressed in Second World War uniform, repeatedly shouting, Where's Annie? When we got to the underground hospital, a man, naked except for his guts spilling out, ran past us, screaming that he wasn't ready to die. Then in the Napoleonic War Tunnels a grubby-faced solider was stomping up and down the corridor yelling at these little boys dressed in rags, who were struggling to carry buckets of water. There was even a ghost hanging around the toilets: a teenage boy banging a large drum next to me as I washed my hands.

I learnt to accept that things were not always what they seemed in my life; like one of those rare sunny winter days when the sun is so low it casts impossibly long shadows, transforming stumpy oak trees into elegant poplars and the washed out greens and yellows of the countryside into semi-Van Gogh landscapes. After reading various books and journals on ghosts, I came to the conclusion that I was adept at seeing things from another dimension just as others were good at knitting or playing football, and for whatever reason, I could tune into the space where the dead were trapped.

I told no-one about what I could see. I saw no point in exposing myself to ridicule. Perhaps if the ghosts had been able to communicate with me and I with them, then I would have done so. Indeed, sometimes I fantasised about having the gift of clairvoyance, of being able to help them pass over, though where 'over' was, I was unsure. My mother worshipped at the new shopping centre and my father, the local pub. And I was deeply suspicious of religion after learning that our neighbours, the Meeks, three worm-torturing boys, would be inheriting the earth. Anyway, a future career as a clairvoyant was ruled out by the fact that most of the ghosts I saw rarely took any notice of me. Instead I became a solicitor.

After qualifying, I moved to London for my first job and began to regularly see the ghost of a young girl in the flat opposite. Ghost number 154, according to my notebook.

Now London's ghosts are a cut above those that frequented the seaside town I grew up in. For a start their ethnicity was far more varied, reflecting the city's cosmopolitan nature. But without sounding too glib their ghostly states were more interesting. Apart from a few drowned smugglers and my household and garden ghosts, my old stomping ground was full of depressed people who had thrown themselves off the cliff to the rocks below. London was inhabited by a far wider range of troubled souls.

For example, just on my short walk to Finsbury Park tube station in the morning I was often accompanied by an elderly Turkish man who had been hit by the 341 bus, swearing and cursing every time one went by. Then there was the handsome teenager with a stab wound to his stomach, slumped on the pavement of Riversdale Road, and the young Jewish lady pushing a pram near the station entrance asking passers-by if they'd seen her baby. In the evening, I'd see families on Green Lanes emerging from their bombed out houses, white-haired and bloodied, staring up at the dust and debris of their homes, ripped apart to expose bedrooms, bathrooms and sitting rooms like trashed dolls' houses.

On every street and every corner lurked some ghost wanting to replay its last few moments after death. At the end of the day, I was pleased to climb up to my top floor flat, shut the door and close the curtains to my other world.

The flat was located in the centre of three identical blocks arranged around a large garden opposite Clissold Park. As such all the flats had a wonderful view across the park and its two lakes which lent them an air of calm despite the constant growling traffic and emergency service sirens on nearby Green Lanes. Best of all, the flat was ghostless.

I was lodging with Mel, a senior lawyer from the company, who'd been seconded to work on a project in Dubai, so I had the place to myself. She'd only lived there for six months and knew as much about the other occupants as I did. I'd moved in during the winter months, leaving for work and returning in the darkness, with little chance to get to know any of the residents, apart from the occasional hurried greeting. But from what I could gather at weekends, they were either affluent young professionals working in the City, or retired, elderly folk like the couple living with ghost number 154. Their flat was in the block next to mine, built at an angle so that if you stood on one side of the balcony doors you could just about see into their front room.

The first time I saw the girl was during the weekend I moved in. I'd been putting up a photo of my parents when I had that eerie feeling you get that someone is watching you. I looked up and there she was standing near the balcony windows, dressed in a dark headscarf and a lime green 1980s-style shell suit staring across the park towards the playground in the distance. Then the elderly man appeared and drew the curtains together. The next time I saw her was the following weekend, early afternoon as I hoovered the sitting room. Again she was standing gazing at the park, the playground beyond, probably where she'd spent most of her childhood running around with her friends. I noticed how big the dark circles were under her eyes. I ducked out of sight as the elderly man appeared with his wife. I didn't want them to see me and think I was a nosey neighbour. After a few moments, I glanced back. The curtains were closed.

I went back to hoovering, trying to shake off the sadness that had settled over me since seeing the ghost. She'd looked exhausted. And I recognised that kind of tiredness as one that accompanies a serious illness like my friend, Ty, had suffered. He'd been diagnosed with leukaemia aged just 12, about the same age as the girl ghost, and had died 18 months later. Though I'd become hardened by seeing so many ghosts, encountering the young always made me think of Ty. I assumed that the girl must have been their daughter and that like my friend, childhood leukaemia, or another cancer had killed her. I imagined the long drawn out trauma that she and her family must have gone through and wondered whether they ever felt her presence, or if they were too consumed by grief to notice.

Over the next few months, I became more and more obsessed by the girl and her parents, or rather with the idea that I could bring them some kind of peace by telling them that she'd never left them. But I only ever saw them once or twice at weekends, as infrequently as their daughter, the father always looked harassed, as if being pursued by swarms of biting and stinging insects; the woman always hidden under a voluminous headscarf, always hurrying behind. I bade them hello each time but they barely acknowledged my presence, sometimes ignoring me.

Death, as I knew from Ty's parents, can be catching. His death killed their marriage. And every time I saw the ghost's parents, I realised they must have died too.

During the spring, I began to the see the ghost daughter more often. The weather had turned unseasonably warm, allowing me to sit on the balcony early evening and at weekends. In fact, I saw her standing overlooking the park so frequently that I began to place my chair with my back to her. But her presence was always so intense I could never resist turning for a moment to acknowledge her. And there she'd be, always standing, away from the door as if scared to be seen, staring out longingly at the park, dressed in the same brown head scarf and shell suit.

The heat wave came to an end on a Sunday evening after the storms it had brewed exploded across London, turning roads into rivers and joining the two lakes opposite. I'd been reading my book in the sitting room when I heard an almighty crash. It sounded like the large recycling bin behind the flats had tipped over, but when I heard the heavy rain against the balcony windows I realised it was just thunder. I broke off from my book and opened the curtains to watch the veiny lightning dance across the sky, the thunder grumbling then rolling towards another neighbourhood.

Out of habit, I glanced over at the ghost flat, one second empty and dark inside, the next lit up by a flash of lightning, the ghost daughter's face up against the doors, staring out at the storm and then turning and catching my eye. I shut the curtains and bolted back onto the sofa, feeling an icy finger on the back of my neck. And as I recalled her face, I realised the dark circles around her eyes weren't caused by illness. They were bruises. The white lightning had shown me something else too. She had opened her mouth as if to speak.

Sleep refused to come that night as I recalled the terrible bruising to her face, my mind whirring with all the new theories as to how she'd died. I only fell asleep in the early hours after settling on a car accident as the probable cause, her parents wracked with guilt for surviving. Or perhaps one of them was the driver of the doomed vehicle. I avoided the balcony for the next few weeks, and kept the curtains closed day and night. Even during the day, I was unable to shake off the image of the bruising to her face. But it wasn't just her injuries that'd unsettled me. I'd had years of bumping into maimed, headless, limbless and bloodied ghosts. This ghost was different, more troubling and I realised it wasn't because of her age either. She'd been gazing out at the storm and had purposefully looked at me and opened her mouth to say something. But what? To tell me something? Give me a message? A warning from beyond the grave?

Whatever it was, I didn't want to know. The more I thought of what had been unsaid, the more monstrous the ghost became. Every night I'd huddle down into my duvet, trying to block out thoughts of her mouth opening into a demonic scream. I was frightened for the first time in my life. Well, could you blame me? After years of being mostly ignored by ghosts, here was one who'd looked directly at me and wanted to make contact. I had to get away. Coincidently, an old school friend had asked a few weeks before if I wanted to move in with her near Old Street and I emailed Mel giving her a month's notice, saying I was finding the flat too lonely. The following week I was on holiday, visiting a friend in Spain for a fortnight. Once back, I'd have just one week left in the flat.

* * *

My friends lived in the countryside outside Cadiz and I spent my holiday playing with their two children, lazing by the pool and drinking too much wine, all helping to blur my memories of the ghost daughter. Gradually, she became less vivid, less terrifying, less real. By the second week I no longer awoke with a jolt, seeing her face pushed up against the balcony door, her red mouth opening into a gaping bottomless chasm capable of swallowing me whole. I'd convinced myself that the stark white of the lightning had created an optical illusion making me think she was staring at me, trying to talk to me.

But my theory melted away as soon as I got off the bus near the flats and saw the elderly Turkish man waiting. I quickly resolved to keep my head down all the way home and not to glance up until I reached the front door.

However, as I turned into the driveway, I found my way barred by two policemen, busily retying 'CRIME SCENE DO NOT CROSS' tape across the entrance.

Beyond I could see two police cars parked outside the flats and a young couple I recognised from my block talking to a woman, who was hurriedly scribbling down their answers in a notebook.

'Excuse me! Can you tell me what's going on?' I called out to the two policemen.

The taller of the two turned and walked away as his radio came to life.

His colleague half smiled in apology and came towards me.

'Been anywhere nice?' he said gesturing at my suitcase.

'Er...Spain. Can you tell me what's going on? I live in number 30.'

He glanced behind him at his colleague, now speaking into the radio, then turned back to me.

'I suppose you'll find out soon enough.'

'Find out what?' I said, suddenly worrying that Mel had returned home and something had happened to her.

The blood began to drain from my face as another thought came; I'd read rare cases of poltergeists who'd harmed the living. Had my ghost neighbour mistaken Mel for me and somehow hurt her?

'A body was found this morning,' he said, pointing behind to the very balcony window I was avoiding.

'The top flat?'

He nodded.

'They've picked him up at Heathrow,' interrupted the tall policeman who'd wandered back.

'He killed his wife?' I wondered aloud, thinking again of how destructive the father's grief must have been, driving him mad over the years and even to murder.

'What? No,' said the tall policeman. 'The wife turned herself in a couple of hours ago. Admitted everything.'

'Admitted what?'

'Murder.'

'Murder?' I repeated in a daze.

'Yeah, we think she was trafficked.'

I looked at him blankly.

'You know, modern day slavery.'

'What his wife?' I said.

I allowed myself a furtive glance at their flat and immediately knew the answer.

Standing on the balcony glaring down at me was my ghost neighbour. Holding my gaze, she moved her head slightly upwards to reveal her neck decorated in livid purple bruises. I felt the bile rising up from my stomach as the policeman's voice cut in.

'No, the girl. She was only 12 or 13, we're not sure. Must have kept her locked up as no-one seems to have seen her.'

Feeling my knees buckling from under me, I tightened my grip around the suitcase handle for support.

'Are you okay?' he asked, untying the tape and gesturing for me to come through.

My heart was thumping so loudly his voice sounded as though it was breaking through from another dimension.

'DC Trilby will need to question you, routine that's all, see if you ever saw her.'

Mrs Shipley's Spinning Wheel

Mum has taken against Mrs Shipley when I visit.

'Showing off. That's all it is,' she says, throwing a well-thumbed copy of *The Gazette* at me.

'Yes, I've seen it already,' I say, catching the paper just before it hits my head.

I open it up anyway, find the offending article and photo on page ten: a thin grey-haired lady sits at her spinning wheel smiling into the camera while an elderly man stands next to her, his hand resting on her shoulder.

I read the photo caption out loud: 'Brian Shipley models cardigan made from friend's Alsatian Artoo Dogtoo.'

'Poor dog. I hope it was dead before they skinned it.'

'It's the way they've written it -.'

'And what kind of stupid name is that for a dog?'

'It's a play on words. A character from *Star Wars*.'

She stares at me then, her mouth turned down as if I've offered her a mouldy lump of cheese to eat.

'What's *Star Wars* got to do with the price of potatoes? And as for poor Mr Shipley. He looks so embarrassed,' she says, glancing out of the window at the house opposite.

'He does not! He's smiling.'

'Grimacing through the pain more like.'

She snatches the paper back.

'Pass me my reading glasses.'

'Where are they?'

'Where they usually are. Over there,' she says, jabbing an arthritic finger vaguely at the dresser.

I scan the shelves. Dinner plates, egg cups, invites, old birthday cards and all the creepy little dolls mum's so fond of glare back at me, defying me to find her glasses.

'Are you blind? There,' she says, pushing herself out of her armchair and retrieving them from a drawer.

'You could have said!'

Mum tuts and rests her glasses on the end of her nose. She settles back into her chair, licks a finger and flicks through the pages. She stops for a few moments to read a story about Mrs Patel, who runs the corner shop, slipping over and breaking both her legs during a freak snowstorm the week before.

'Serves her right,' she mumbles before searching through the pages again.

'Mum!'

'Shhh...I'm trying to concentrate. Aha! Let's have a proper look, shall we?'

She irons out page ten with a fist and squints at the photo of Mrs Shipley.

'Who does she think she is? Showing off like that.'

I dig my fingers into the back of her faded brown armchair, searching and finding my familiar worry hole.

'Mum, she's not showing off. It's an article appealing for dog fur donations.'

'Dog. Fur. Donations. I've heard everything now.'

'What's wrong with that? People make jumpers out of all sorts of animal hair. Why not a dog's?'

'And she's always got that poor Mr Shipley fetching and carrying the spinning wheel to and from the car. Poor man.'

'Cup of tea?' I ask, escaping to the kitchen where the familiar smell of Mum's special brew greets me.

'Yes, and while you're there, check the saucepan, will you? If it's boiling, turn it off.'

I'm pleased to find the kitchen relatively clean: there are a few bread crumbs on the sideboard and several orangey-brown blobs decorate the tiles where the bubbling goo has exploded. I give the contents a stir, turn it off and wait for the kettle to boil, trying to remember a time when Mum hadn't taken against something or somebody. Last week it'd been Mrs Patel who'd messed up her *Woman's World* magazine delivery, and the week before that my brother, who'd failed to visit her for two weeks, even though he was holidaying in Spain.

Mrs Shipley had always skirted the edges of the top 20 people/things Mum liked to complain about ever since she'd married Mr Shipley six months before. I wondered if she was jealous: Dad had died of a heart attack 20 years ago and Mum hadn't met anyone since. I couldn't help wondering if she secretly harboured a romantic longing for the kindly octogenarian, or was offended that he could move on so quickly after the death of his wife, Mary, two years before. Not that Mum had anything nice to say about her either.

When I come back into the room, Mum's standing behind her armchair, peering out across the row of terraced houses opposite.

'Give us a hand and help me push it closer,' she says.

'Shall I fetch a pair of binoculars?'

'Don't be silly.'

I put the tea down onto the coffee table and edge the chair closer to the window.

'Stop! That's perfect,' she says.

She settles herself back into the chair as I spot a smartly dressed lady with a short grey bob emerge from the house opposite, followed by the famous spinning wheel.

'See, she's got him at it again!' she says, rising up from the chair and yanking back the yellowing nylon net curtains.

We watch Mrs Shipley open up the boot of her old black Saab as Mr Shipley shuffles along, legs bent at the knees as he struggles to carry the offending spinning wheel.

'I'll go and give them a hand.'

'You'll do no such thing, young lady. Sit down,' says Mum, grabbing my arm.

'Mum!'

'I don't want you going anywhere near her.'

'Mum!'

'There's more to her than meets the eye,' she says, releasing me.

'You could say that about most people.'

I rub my wrist. Her grip is still surprisingly strong.

'No, I've always felt it with that woman. Ever since she wheedled her way into poor Mr Shipley's life.'

'What do you mean 'wheedled her way into his life'?'

'Well, she just appeared out of nowhere. For all we know she could be one of those mail order brides you read about.'

'They're from Thailand not Dover.'

'Who knows what you can order on that dark web these days. Anyway, I reckon she's up to something.'

'Like what?' I say, watching Mr Shipley slam the boot and walk towards the passenger's side.

'You wouldn't believe me if I told you. It'd make your toes curl.'

'Mum! You used to be good friends with Mo when she first moved in.'

'I never liked her.'

'She used to come round and play cards with you and Betty-Jo but you didn't like the fact that she always won.'

'Only because she cheated. Messed around with the cards. Hid them up her sleeves. Put Betty-Jo right off coming round. That's why she went back to America.'

'Oh come on! You know full well that Betty-Jo went back to look after her sister because she was going blind.'

'Then she threatened me. I bet you didn't know that.'

'Yes, you've told me several dozen times. In great detail. It was over parking and she didn't threaten you. She just asked you not to park outside her house otherwise Mr Shipley, with his arthritis, finds it difficult to carry the spinning wheel to and from the car: something we have just witnessed.'

'And about her bloody cat.'

'Well you shouldn't have thrown the stones at it like that. Poor animal.'

'It was messing in my garden. Horrible thing too. It's got fangs on it like you've never seen before. Like a sabre-toothed tiger. It's not normal for a cat, you know. And I bet you didn't know I caught it in the kitchen. It must have sneaked in when I put out the bins. Spat at me like it was some kind of fiend from Hell. And it bit my ankle.'

'Twist? He's as soft as anything. Always rubbing himself up against my ankles.'

'How can you say that?' she says, shaking her body as if she had a shiver running down her spine. 'Gives me the willies the way it creeps around and suddenly appears out of nowhere.'

'That's what cats do.'

'It even looks like her with its big ugly amber eyes and all that grey fur.'

'Oh, Mum.'

'Where does she take the bloody spinning wheel anyway?'

We watch the Saab drive off down the road.

'As I said before if you'd read the article properly, then you'll have known that she gives spinning classes at the community centre twice a week.'

'They're at it more than twice a week. So what else is she up to, I ask you? Spinning her evil spells, no doubt.'

'Mum! She probably gives private lessons. Who knows and who really cares? Can we just stop talking about her? Please.'

I plug in the Hoover, desperate for its whir to block out any-more accusations about Mrs Shipley and her spinning wheel.

My foot hovers over the power switch just as she starts again.

'Oh, and did I tell you?' she shouts across the room.

I take in a deep breath and breathe out slowly. I only visit once a week and have an hour to clean the house before I need to pick up Jo from football.

'Tell me what?' I say, poking my head around the door.

'That Sandy Kavanagh moved out.'

'Yesssss.'

'She was desperate to leave. Next door but one to that Shipley woman. What do you think about that?'

'Not a lot.'

'She couldn't bear it anymore.'

'Bear what?' I say, sloping around the door and leaning against the door frame waiting for the inevitable.

'Mrs Shipley. Who do you think?'

'Er, actually no. She's moved in with Karen, her daughter in Dorset. Remember? I told you. I'm friends with her on Facebook.'

'She only tells people that because she's scared of Shipley.'

'No, because it's true.'

Mum takes a sip of her tea, raising her eyebrows.

'Bet Karen didn't mention anything about the screaming at night?'

'Oh, for goodness sake! What screaming?'

'Sandy thought it was the telly at first and asked nicely if they could turn it down. And it stopped.'

'Well then....'

'For a while. And then it started up again. Young girls screaming. Men shouting and swearing. Banging on walls. Thumping up and down the stairs and on the floorboards. So she went round again. That Shipley woman said it was a violent TV drama. Mr Shipley waiting for a new hearing aid *apparently.*'

'There you go. Big mystery solved.'

'She couldn't wait to leave. Always lots of strange people banging on her door at all sorts of odd times.'

'What Karen's mum?'

'No, silly, Shipley.'

'Yes. They're called friends,' I mutter.

'Ha, ha. Very funny. I wouldn't like to have friends like them.'

'What exactly is wrong with their friends? How can you complain about a group of OAP visitors?'

'OAP visitors? That lot aren't OAPs. And if they are, they're not from round here. They only ever visit when it gets dark and they're always dressed in black. Some of them even wear cloaks with hoods. And I never see them leave.'

I take in another deep breath and unclench my teeth.

'You're just seeing things. Anyway, they probably leave when you're not being a nosy neighbour.'

'I am not a nosy neighbour. I take an interest in the neighbourhood. There's a huge difference.'

'If you say so. Anyway, can we stop talking about your neighbours. I've been waiting for you to ask about Jo, your grandson. Remember him?'

'I thought you didn't want me to talk about people?'

'Mum!'

'That boy leaving him alone now?' she says.

Her eyes wander over to the dresser. I can't stop mine from following and draw them away quickly but not before I register the rows and rows of mum's horrible dolls, lined up like a parade of battle-scarred soldiers.

'Yes, you know he is. He's been off school for ages now. Doctors don't know what's wrong with him. I kind of feel sorry for him.'

She sips her tea and pulls a face.

'Sugar?'

'Doctor?'

'Sugar.'

I fetch the bowl and scoop up a small teaspoon.

'Anyway, I wanted to tell you about Jo and his GSCEs,' I say swiping the sugar bowl out of reach.

'Oh, he's not old enough, surely?'

'He's 16.'

'He'll be taking them next year then?'

'He took them months ago, mum. He's got his results this week. Three A*s, 4 As and two Bs.'

'Shame about the Bs.'

'Mum!'

'I'm joking. Very pleased for him. Send him my congratulations,' she says, stirring her tea until it's a mini whirlpool. 'You know poor Mrs Rainsford died.'

'Yes, three months ago, mum.'

'Private ambulance came and took her away in a body bag. Put me right off my lunch.'

'Well, I'm sure she'd be mortified to think she'd -.'

'She lived in number 21, right next to the Shipleys.'

'So your conclusion is that the coroner's wrong. She didn't die of a heart attack. Mrs Shipley killed her.'

'Well, now there's a thought,' she says, glancing up at me in mock horror, as if such a thought had never crossed her mind.

'I suppose she beat her to death with her spinning wheel?'

'Don't be ridiculous, Eleanor.'

Mum looks at me through her glasses, the way she used to when I'd done something naughty as a child, her blue eyes so magnified I can see all the tiny blood vessels in the whites of her eyes.

'Oh, *I'm* being silly, am I?'

'You're getting carried away like you used to as a little girl. Always taking things too far. Anyway, what about Maggie's old house, number 25? It's been on the market for a year now. No-one wants to move in next to that Mrs Shipley.'

'Because it's overpriced.'

'Nothing to do with those dark shadows then?'

I cross my arms, feeling like I've been zapped back to my teenage years.

'Really.'

'Yes, it's true. Flittering across the windows. Winged creatures and tall figures mostly but I've seen little stooped ones too. I've been watching all these young couples coming and going all week. Turn up all excited thinking they're going to get a bargain and five minutes later, they're back on the street, white as bleached bones. Can't wait to get away.'

'Mum!'

'It's that Shipley woman and her spinning wheel. I bet you she's going to buy it up for a song and sell it for a fat profit.'

I glance at the kitchen clock. Only another 40 minutes and I can leave.

I go back into the dining room and stamp my foot down on the Hoover. Its growling is as welcome as a cool sea breeze on a hot day and I suck up cobwebs dangling high in the ceilings along with their skinny-legged spinners.

* * *

I get round the house with ten minutes to spare after I'd put all the cleaning equipment away.

'Another tea?' I call as I shove the Hoover back under the stairs.

'Why not. Fetch us a biscuit too, will you?' Mum says. 'Usual place.'

I put the kettle on and sigh. Mum's saucepan of stew has disappeared but she hasn't bothered to clean away after herself. While the kettle boils, I scrub away at the little blobs stuck to the rings before retrieving the packet of chocolate digestives from the casserole dish, a rubbish hiding place for childhood treats that had now become the official biscuit container.

As I close the kitchen blind, I catch a glimpse of an over-furred grey cat landing on the windowsill. I watch Twist leap onto the recycling bin before springing onto the fence and disappearing. I go into the sitting room and place the mug on the coffee table next to Mum's saucepan of goop, lying on the open pages of *The Gazette*.

Mum's knobbly fingers have already turned orange as she sculpts a lump of her vile gunk into a shapeless figure; a head stuck on a blob for a torso with two fat arms and legs poking out. She holds it next to Mrs Shipley's newsprint face as if comparing it for likeness.

'Perfect,' she says. 'Go and fetch the pins from the usual place, will you.'

The story was adapted as a play and performed by Get Over It Productions at the Chiswick Playhouse, London 2019.

Slugs and Other Beasts

When I come down in the morning I find the following message stuck to the kitchen door: WARNING. INJURED SLUG AT LARGE. ENTER AT YOUR OWN RISK.

I rip the note off, remembering last week's hideous seven-incher. I'd come into the kitchen just in time to see it rear up on Jim's shoulder, ready to sink its yellow fangs into his neck while he dished out the kid's beans on toast.

It must have jumped him while he put away his bike in the garage. Then slithered up his back, leaving a negligee of slime, decorating his best suit. Jim'd been lucky not to receive a fever-inducing bite. He'd whipped off his jacket, leapt out of the back door, and smacked the slug repeatedly against the outside wall. From the safety of the conservatory me and the kids watched it drop to the floor, its body curling into a mad smile, reminding me of one of Arthur's joke plastic moustaches.

Jim flashed a mouth of rarely seen and surprisingly white teeth, wiping his brow as if he'd slain a tiger. Arthur cheered. Sadie buried her face into the folds of my dress, clinging to me as we went outside. After kicking its body into the nettles, Jim put his arm around my shoulders. For a moment, it felt like the old days. Then I remembered and walked inside.

I stare at Jim's scrawl, wondering how the slug managed to get into the house, and which kitchen implement Jim used to attack it with. Then another darker thought comes: perhaps the slug he'd killed last week wasn't actually dead and had returned to wreak revenge.

'Don't be so stupid,' I say out loud.

'Mum, what's Arthur doing?' Sadie shouts from upstairs, her footsteps getting closer.

From the top step, she peers down at me through sleepy slivers of jade.

'Arthur's still in bed. I was talking to myself.'

We stare at each other, both waiting for the other to move.

'Why are you holding a torn cornflakes packet?'

'It's just a note from Daddy...time to get dressed and wake Arthur as you go, please,' I say as she thumps back upstairs.

I don't have much time to act. I need to make the kids' sandwiches and breakfast. I put my ear to the door and listen for any sounds of slithering. All is quiet, except for the comforting tick-tock of the cuckoo clock.

I grab my mobile and ring Jim who's on his way to work. The call goes straight to voicemail. I open my mouth, favoured expletives ready to explode but force myself to end the call. We'd promised the counsellor we'd be kinder to each other.

Just above me, I hear feet pounding down from the top floor. I have to move. Fast.

I fling open the kitchen door, and scan the floor and work surfaces.

All clear.

I jerk my head up at the ceiling, recalling how they sometimes ambush their victims from above. But, thankfully, there's not a glistening trail in sight.

I creep towards the bin at the far side of the kitchen mindful of the Public Health adverts warning us of slug dangers: how they can squeeze through the tiniest of entry points and have a chameleon's ability to merge with your orange sofa one moment, only to vanish into the kitchen's cream tiles the next. But the most disturbing fact of all is this; they work in gangs shimmying up bins, using the weight of their fat bodies to buck up and down on top of the lids to release catches and nest inside.

I yank the bin out of its dark corner, bracing myself to face a jellied nest writhing around in panic at being disturbed. A slice of cucumber, its pips forming a disappointed world-weary face, and a mouldy eye stump of a carrot top stare back.

The only tell-tale sign is the slimy trail winding its way across the conservatory's purple rug. I sprint to the kitchen sink cupboard to find the can of *Reveal*, a spray that shows up their trails. Pressing down hard on the nozzle, a cloud of fine mist splutters out, releasing a hiss belonging to a pathetic snake.

'Jim!'

Had he always been this thoughtless, I think? Had love blinded me to it when we first met nearly 20 years ago? It was a time when garden slugs were a harmless inconvenience, littering the patio and devouring plants: six years before a dozen Giant Amazonian Creeper slugs had escaped from the town's disgraced Danos Institute. Scientists had been trying to harvest the supposed anti-ageing properties of their trails after a youthful-looking Indian tribe were discovered deep in the Amazon. The tribe's elder had joked they used the famous Creepers' slime as a moisturizer and the Danos Institute believed him, going into overdrive to be the first laboratory to produce a miracle face cream. But as soon as the trials revealed the slime contained zero age-defying properties, they allowed the Creepers to slither into the Kent countryside.

* * *

Half way to school, I notice Sadie's no longer walking beside us. We turn to see her stooping down, examining something in the road.

As we retrace our steps, I see her bottom lip's sticking out, a sure sign that tears are pooling.

'It's a WheelieHam, Mummy. It's still alive.'

I roll my eyes to the white clouds floating above, wishing I could join them.

'Bloody Danos Institute.'

I kneel beside her to get a closer look. Then turn away. Its body has separated from its wheels. A little stream of blood is pumping from an exposed artery, painting its beige fur red.

'Oh, sweetheart. There's nothing we can do.'

'But someone may run him over.'

'Bit late for that.'

'Arthur!' I say, cuddling Sadie. 'I'll deal with it later.'

'What? Bring it home?'

'No, darling. It won't survive.'

'Can you ring the council then? Ella's dad got them to take away the one that -.'

'Their cat mauled,' interrupts Arthur.

Sadie thumps her brother's arm. I take her bloodied fingers in mine, wondering what to do with the WheelieHam. The so-called living toys had proved popular with kids for the first few months, until parents complained their wonky cartilage wheels left them prone to accidents and injuries. They began to be abandoned in the streets and shortly afterwards, the Danos Institute went bankrupt. It'd been left to Folkestone and Hythe Council to dispose of the injured and dead.

* * *

Later that morning, after contacting the council, I try ringing Jim again and leave a message.

'It's me. I've killed a WheelieHam. It was horrible. Oh, and I can't find the slug,' I say, feeling tiny pin pricks of annoyance rushing over me.

It was yet another habit of Jim's never to answer his mobile during the day, though one, I expect, he hadn't extended to Celine, the work colleague he'd had an affair with.

I rip off a piece of kitchen roll and wipe away my tears, trying not to think of the WheelieHam's soft brown eyes pleading for mercy as I smashed the hammer down on its head. I'd only managed to kill it by substituting its bloodied face for Jim's.

I'm just about to open the garage to put its body out of sight when the WheelieHam collector pulls up outside. I'd imagined a squat rat-catcher type wearing a flat cap over his podgy head, a blood-soaked sack slung over his shoulder. But coming towards me is a man in his 20s with brilliant green eyes lined with dark lashes. His brown hair is shaved to one side to reveal a tattoo of a skull and crossbones like the WheelieHam's very own grim reaper.

'I found him in the road,' I say, holding out the plastic bag.

'There's hardly any left. Collectors and taxidermists pay a fortune if they're alive or dead,' he says, taking the bag and yanking it open to look inside.

He pulls a face and closes the bag quickly.

'There'll be no takers for this little fella.'

'Must have been a bus,' I say.

I feel the blush of my lie running up my neck. It'll reach my face any time soon so I disappear inside to fetch my purse for a tip.

When I return, he's holding the mashed contents at arm's length, placing it carefully in his van, emblazoned with a cartoon picture of a Creeper looking up worriedly as a giant boot looms above it.

I give him a £5 note and quickly tell him about Jim and the injured slug.

'He's been so busy at work, you see,' I add, suddenly feeling disloyal.

Together we search the house for all the obvious hiding places. However, as we check each room, my mind quickly wanders away from the dangers posed by the Creeper to what Jim would do if I were to have a revenge affair with the WheelieHam collector? How I'd relish telling him my lover would never leave me and the kids alone with an injured slug, or use up a full can of *Reveal* without replacing it.

After a cup of tea, the collector declares the house Creeper-free.

'Or if there's been one, it's probably scarpered,' he says, gesturing at the cuckoo clock. 'What most people don't realise is that birds are their natural predators.'

'Really?' I say, glancing up at the clock, doubting very much that even the most myopic Creeper could be scared off a tiny mechanical bird.

I text Jim as soon as he leaves.

The collector has taken the WheelieHam. He checked the house and thinks you're mistaken re: Creeper.

I smile to myself knowing there was nothing Jim found more irritating than being proved wrong. And as I go to fetch the kids from school, I constantly glance at my mobile, expecting him to rise to the bait any moment.

But by 5pm he still hasn't replied. I'm not unduly worried: Jim had promised the counsellor he'd be home by 6pm to cook tea for his *Task of the Week*. So I busy myself with cleaning the kitchen floor to banish the sickly burnt toast smell of *Reveal*.

By 6.30pm, with no sign of Jim, I pour myself a large glass of wine and cook the kids' tea.

'Naughty Daddy,' says Arthur as the cuckoo scoots out to announce the first stroke of 7 o'clock.

I turn to see Arthur and Sadie staring at me with chocolate mousse beards and moustaches.

'He's probably in the pub,' says Arthur, before licking his bowl clean.

After putting the kids to bed, I down two more glasses of wine and try ringing Jim again. As much as I hate to admit it, my ten-year-old son is probably right.

Sorry, forgot to tell you. It was so and so's birthday or bla-de-bla's leaving do. Be back by 10pm, he'll say.

But 10pm always turns into 1am when he crashes through the front door, filling the house with his poisonous fumes, or the following evening, with some excuse about missing the last train.

* * *

Any sleep I manage that night is laced with disturbing dreams about Jim running off with numerous women; all composites of people we know, including a knife-wielding female version of the WheelieHam collector.

In the morning, Arthur and Sadie run into the room to wake me, glancing at Jim's unslept in half of the bed.

'He left early,' I say.

I gulp back my tears and hurry downstairs to make breakfast. It was obvious Jim didn't want to make a go of it, even though he'd been the one to beg for my forgiveness.

As I herd the kids out of the door to school, the phone rings.

'Daddy!' says Sadie.

'He can wait,' I say.

But she's already run back inside.

I follow and snatch the phone from her.

'About time!'

'Hello Mrs Hall?'

I recognise the school secretary's voice immediately.

'Sorry. I thought -,' I say.

'Just to remind you that Arthur needs his bike and helmet for Cycle Club.'

The kids wait on the pavement watching ants pouring out of a crack while I fetch Arthur's bike. I heave my shoulder against the garage door but it won't budge. Jim must have knocked down the bag of beach toys on his way out again and they're blocking the door. I throw myself against it in frustration, hot tears ready to burst. With a bang, it opens three feet or so, giving me enough room to crawl under and clear the toys out of the way.

But as I bend down and peer in, I can see there are no beach toys blocking the door. Instead, gloopy strands of slime hang from the rafters, pooling onto the concrete floor.

And in the far corner, Jim is slumped against the wall encased in a transparent gel, incubating thousands of pulsating, yellow eggs.

The Spinning Monkeys

I'd only got to touch it once before Grandma hid it away. So as soon as she died, I began plotting to get my grubby little hands on it. The spinning monkeys or praxinoscope, as I was later to learn its correct name, had stood at the back of Grandma's glass cabinet guarded by a beige blur of Wimsey dogs and cats.

She'd taken it out after our nagging; by turning a shiny metal handle the static pictures of monkeys began tumbling over each other at great speed. Its simplicity was mesmerising. For those of you who have never come across a praxinoscope, let me explain. It's a circular device dating back to the Victorian era containing strips of pictures around the inner circle of a cylinder and another inner circle of mirrors, allowing you to see the reflection of the moving pictures. It was early animation and there was something magically fluid about the way the monkeys spilled over one another. Grandma had snatched it up after a few spins and returned it to the back of the cabinet, warning us never to touch it without her permission.

A few weeks later, it was the summer holidays. Our parents had to work most days, and me and my younger sister by two years, Kate, often spent our summer at Grandma's, an old farmhouse just outside Oxford. Grandma bought and sold antiques for a living and, as a consequence, the rooms were jammed full of curiosities. Every time we visited we'd discover something new: an overstuffed weasel which looked as though it'd eaten too many ice creams, ration books full of stamps for measly amounts of butter and sugar, or the strange oil painting we found under our mother's old bed, depicting four Victorian children, no older than us, smoking and playing cards.

On the first day of the holidays we'd positioned ourselves in front of the TV, next to the cabinet and the object of our desire. Grandma was due any moment to bring our mid-morning snack of a biscuit and orange squash. After she placed the tray onto a battered old coffee table, I struck.

'Thanks, Grandma. Can we play with the -?' I asked but she'd already closed the door behind her.

I glanced at Kate who rolled her eyes and gestured with a flick of her head for me to follow. I got up and scampered after Grandma.

I found her in the kitchen, at the sink, wrestling her hands into a pair of faded yellow washing up gloves. I stood next to her and tugged gently at her apron, repeating our request.

'We'll be really careful,' I pleaded.

'I wondered how long it'd take you,' she said, bending down so her face was level with mine. I was so close I could see the broken red veins scribbled over her cheeks.

'Now listen to me. It's not a toy. It's far too precious to play with. You see, there's not many of them left in the world.'

'I promise we'll be really, really careful. You can come and sit with us and -,'

The sound of tyres crunching on gravel made us both look up.

Grandma pulled off her gloves, smoothed down her hair, and walked towards the front door. I peeked my head into the hallway, watching the postman's red van turning multi-coloured through the stained glass window as it pulled up outside.

It was our one chance. She often took ages signing for various items she'd bought. I sprinted back into the sitting room. But Kate had beaten me to it. She was holding up the praxinoscope like a trophy, the Wimsey guards lying scattered around her feet. She put it down on the sofa, took my hand and placed it over hers, and together we turned the handle. The monkeys managed half a dozen spins before I felt a sharp slap across my ear.

'I told you not to touch it!'

I began howling. No one had ever hit me before. I put my hand to my ear to ease the stinging. Through my tears, I watched the spinning monkeys rising through the air as Grandma grabbed it, the shock of the slap turning the monkeys' playful grins into twisted sneers, their innocent tumbling into pinching, slapping and punching.

'It's going into the attic,' she said, carrying it out of the room and kicking the door shut behind her.

I refused to look at Grandma for the rest of the day. She didn't try to console me. As far as she was concerned, I'd deserved the slap. Of course, I told Mum as soon as she arrived, though she had little sympathy.

'Didn't you used to play with it?' Kate'd asked Mum on the way home.

'Just the once when she first bought it. It gave me the creeps, to be honest, the way the horses' ears were pinned back, pulling mean faces, bucking and rearing.'

'Horses? Has she got another?' asked Kate.

'Only the one as far as I know.'

'This one has mean monkeys,' I said.

'Really?' said Mum. 'I suppose I could have just imagined the horses. It was a horrible time. Not long after my friend, Sally, fell off her pony and broke her neck. I'd always been jealous of her and I felt guilty I'd somehow caused her to fall off.'

She caught my eye in the driver's mirror. 'But it was all a long time ago. Maybe Sally died before and I'm getting confused.'

* * *

Over the years the memory faded, occasionally stirred by a reference to a praxinoscope in a book, and I'd think about the spinning monkeys banished to the attic.

However, it was only on Grandma's death bed that the memory of the smack came flooding back. As I held her still cold waxy hand, I couldn't quite connect the knobbly rheumatic fingers with the same strong hand that'd delivered such a sharp slap. I could almost feel my left ear stinging at the memory. I looked across at Kate. I opened my mouth to remind her of the spinning monkeys. But something made me stop; I realised I didn't want her to remember. After all, she'd been the one to defy Grandma, yet I was the one who was punished. It was a scenario played out again and again throughout our childhood and through adulthood, where she landed plum jobs and two wealthy husbands, despite breaking up marriages and trampling over anyone in her way. Life was a game to Kate.

I quickly made up my mind over Grandma's stroke-ravaged body. If Kate mentioned the praxinoscope, I'd acknowledge the incident by saying how could I forget taking the slap? And as her only child had left home, wouldn't it be nice for my two to enjoy playing with the spinning monkeys? If she didn't, then I would take it at the first opportunity. Only then would I tell her, presenting my custodianship as a desire to please her nephews. However, I needn't have fretted. Kate mentioned nothing of the spinning monkeys. She'd clearly forgotten about them.

Two days after the funeral, Mum summoned us to Grandma's house. We were to take what we wanted before the house clearance company arrived the following day. I knew Kate was often tardy with her timekeeping but I couldn't risk her being early for once and laying claim to the praxinoscope - if Grandma hadn't sold it. No doubt, Kate would ask Mum what time I was getting there, so I'd lied.

'You're early! We've only just got here ourselves,' said Mum as she answered the door.

'I forgot I have to pick up the boys from gymnastics today.'

I walked into the hall, inhaling its familiar damp smell and noticed how much Mum had aged over the last few weeks. Purple circled her red-rimmed eyes. Her healthy glow had been replaced by a doughy complexion.

'Still not sleeping?'

'No, it's been horrible going through her things,' she said, picking up a small cardboard box from the hall table.

She shook it under my nose. Dozens of little pottery dogs and cats jostled for space. I stroked her shoulder.

'I suppose we better get on,' she said.

'I'll take the attic, shall I?'

'Your sister's already up there.'

'What? When you said 'we' I thought you meant Dad and you.'

'No, he had to work. And Kate was early for the first time in her life. She offered to do the attic last night when she rang. She was asking about those spinning monkeys Grandma hid away.'

'Did she now?' I said putting my bag down in the hallway. 'Best go and help her.'

'Well, I thought you could -.'

I didn't wait to hear the rest of her sentence. I took the stairs two at a time and came to the attic ladder. I was about to shout up but stopped, berating myself for forgetting how Kate'd always been one step ahead of me. I remembered the scratching sounds we'd heard when we slept over. Kate'd convinced me they were being made by demons scuttling around in the attic, playing with the praxinoscope. I'd often lie awake, listening to Kate's snores, imagining the demons now bored with the spinning monkeys, clawing their way through the ceiling, until the day the tree surgeon lopped off the branches of the cherry tree and the scratching ceased.

I crept up the ladder, listening for sounds of movement above. There was a few shuffling noises and I paused half way as I heard what I thought was giggling. It stopped as suddenly as it'd started and I began climbing again. When I reached the third from last rung, I stuck my head through the door.

'Hello?'

Kate was standing on two beams, clutching the praxinoscope to her, wobbling from side to side.

'What the hell, Sarah. You could have killed me!'

She quickly regained her balance.

'Ah, you've found the spinning monkeys.'

'It's called a praxinoscope, actually. I've done quite a bit of research into them over the years,' she said.

'Whatever it's called I thought the kids would like to play with it,' I said climbing up the rest of the ladder, noticing how the attic was remarkably empty considering how many antiques Grandma used to hoard.

I stood next to the attic door, one leg on its edge and another planted firmly on a beam.

'Grandma was right; they really are very valuable. It's not suitable for children, especially *your* boys. You know how they like to break everything,' she said.

'They do not like to break everything! They came to yours once and it was an accident.'

'*It* was a rare Wedgewood vase Grandma had gifted me. Anyway, she'd hate them playing with it. Remember how she smacked us?'

'Smacked me! You got it out and I got into trouble. Sound familiar?'

'Oh, poor hard done by Sarah.'

I took my foot off the side of the attic door and stepped across to the next beam so I was standing next to Kate.

'And your memory's very selective. Anyway, I've told them all about it. I said I'd bring it back today.'

I held out my hands to take the praxinoscope.

Kate blew a layer of dust off the handle and I watched the particles dance in a shaft of sunlight sneaking through a gap in the roof tiles.

'I was thinking how pretty it'll look on my mantelpiece,' she said, turning the handle and smiling.

The monkeys picked up speed, each one separate at first before tumbling over one another. I looked at Kate, her face a mask of pure smugness, then back at the monkeys, their features becoming more twisted and demonic, yet familiar as they morphed into me and my sister. And before I knew it, I was falling fast, my head cracking against the side of the attic door just as I realised Kate had won again.

First published in the Toys and Games issue, Here Comes Everyone.

The Annual General Meeting of the East Kent Macumba Society

'They'll not be welcome here again,' says Dad as we watch the convoy of cars speed away.

They approach the bend, their brake lights flashing red like devil eyes. I wish I could believe Dad but I can't. So I scrunch mine shut, willing our departing guests to crash and die. When I open them again, the cars have disappeared. Dad sighs heavily.

'Shall I start with the sitting room?' I ask.

'Most definitely not after last year's fiasco,' says Dad. 'You can start on the top floor. I've already had a quick look and it's not too bad, considering.'

I drag my feet along the corridor, slowing outside the sitting room door, my hand reaching for the door knob.

'Ryan James!' says Dad, smacking my hand away. 'We've got a lot to do before your mother's home.'

'What if I find another?'

'Pick it up with a plastic bag and put it in the wheelbarrow at the bottom of the garden. I'll dispose of it as soon as I get a chance. Now, don't forget to wear gloves. Work your way around and we'll meet on the first floor.'

'On my own? But that's six bedrooms... five en-suites.'

'Less complaining and more cleaning, young man. Your mother's back at 6pm and you know how upset she got last time.'

I stomp up the stairs. How could I forget? The screaming. The tears. Then the side effects from the anti-depressants.

'She shouldn't go on her stupid anniversary trip then should she?' I shout.

'Have some respect, Ryan James. Your mother needs a break after all her hard work,' Dad yells up the stairs.

A bucket, mop, hoover and cleaning backpack are waiting for me on the first floor landing. I take a deep breath, wondering all sorts of bad thoughts. Like why Dad thinks it's okay to get his 14-year-old son involved with the East Kent Macumba Society but not his adult wife, who swans off every year to a spa with Auntie Sarah to mark Grandpa's death. And exactly what do aromatherapy massages and colonic irrigation have to do with remembering Grandpa anyway? Dad packs her off every year under the pretence of caring about Grandpa. But he knows she wouldn't put up with our guests for five minutes.

I don't expect the top floor to be too bad and find the first three rooms, two singles and a double, practically spotless. I'm guessing most of the mess is going to be on the first floor where all the drumming and shrieking was coming from. But as I open the door to the master bedroom, I shrink back. My eyes take in the sea of dead flowers scattered over the carpet and bed. I half expect the Bride of Frankenstein to stumble out of the en-suite.

There's a horrible smell too. Like a public toilet. I pinch my nostrils shut, steeling myself for having to clear up other people's urine.

'Everything all right up there?' calls Dad.

'Piss and dead flowers,' I shout.

'Language, Ryan James!'

I wrestle on the rubber gloves and snap the medical mask over my nose, feeling myself prickle with injustice: my language was nothing compared to what our guests got up to.

I begin with the flowers, picking up red and yellow rose petals and watch them crumble in my fingers, imagining our guests furtively harvesting dead flowers from cemeteries. Three large vases, I'd brought up the night before, are lying among the flowers, the yellow water creating multicoloured ponds in the swirly carpet, as well as the bad smell.

I strip the sheets. Apart from a few springy pubic hairs, I don't find anything else unpleasant. The bathroom too is surprisingly clean and I give it a quick going over with a cloth. I remember Mum's hysterical screaming and check behind the curtains and under the armchair, mini sofa and the bed. But all is clear and I take my cleaning equipment to the next room, a small double where the bedspread is cradling an imprint of two bodies. I clear several Brahama beer bottles from the sideboard and empty the dregs in the sink, wrinkling my nose at the yeasty stench as the golden liquid fizzes down the plug hole.

The next room is in much the same condition; one lone body shape in foetal pose imprinted on the bedspread. Although the bed hasn't been slept in, I strip it anyway as I know Dad will send me back if I don't. I use the mop to fish a pair of men's underpants from under the bed. They're emblazoned with a colour photo of the Sugar Loaf Mountain. I quickly shove them to the bottom of the bin bag, shuddering at the thought of Dad adopting them as he is prone to do with guests' unclaimed clothing.

'Dad?' I shout as I walk down the stairs, trying to carry the hoover, mop, bucket and cleaning backpack at the same time.

It's too much. The hoover slips out of my hand and dramatically rolls down the stairs like it's a stunt hoover. I hurry after it but when I get to the bottom of the stairs, Dad is standing there dressed in Mum's pink cleaning piny, green rubber-gloved hands on hips, the hoover lying at his feet.

'I suppose it'd had enough of the mess and threw itself down the stairs?'

'It just slipped.'

'Be more careful. Hoovers don't grow on trees, you know.'

'Really? Not even suc-amore trees?'

Dad mock clips me round the ear

'Come on! We haven't got time to mess around. I need some young legs to pop to the larder and fetch the stain remover. Blood's a bugger to get out of the curtains.'

I jog downstairs and glance out of the larder window at the garden, remembering the night before. We were sleeping in Grandpa's old flat over the garage and while Dad snored the night away, I kept being woken up by shouting, drumming and a few screams of what I hoped was delight. I couldn't get back to sleep so I made myself a cup of tea and sat on the balcony with the man on the moon keeping me company. A few moments later, we watched the Brazilians spill out of the French windows onto the terrace, where after a lot of whispering, they gathered in a circle.

I'd quickly grabbed Grandpa's binoculars and watched a woman in her 60s, dressed in a long white robe and turban, waving her arms up and down. I recognised her from breakfast. She'd complained about her fried eggs being undercooked. I zoomed in as she went up to Nelson, the man who organised the AGM, and started wafting her hands around him as if he'd done a big stinky fart and she was trying to dissipate the smell. I felt embarrassed for him. But he just stood there, eyes closed, not at all fazed by being so publicly humiliated. She then moved onto Nelson's latest girlfriend, a twenty-something, olive-skinned woman with closely cropped bleached blonde hair, who again stood impassively as the woman went about her wafting.

But the weird thing was after she'd wafted five or six people, there was a strange greyish froth flowing from of her mouth and down her chin. By the time she'd finished wafting the entire circle of 30, her mouth was pouring with the stuff like she'd swallowed a box of washing powder. She then threw herself onto the lawn and rolled around as if her robes were on fire. I waited for someone to kneel down and help but they just stood there watching her convulsing as if such behaviour was an every-day occurrence. Perhaps it was in Brazil, but as we were on the outskirts of Dover, I thought I'd better wake Dad and call an ambulance. However, just as I was about to get up, she sat up, wiped the foam away with her robes and started chatting away as if nothing had happened.

I grab the stain remover and glance at the kitchen clock. We only had another three hours before Mum came home so I take the stairs two at a time, shouting for Dad.

All the bedroom and bathroom doors are closed. I knock on each just in case he's cleaning inside. But there's no sound of scrubbing or running water. Then, out of the corner of my eye, I spot a flash of fuchsia out of the landing window. It's Dad wheeling the barrow down to the end of the garden.

I sprint after him, and get there in time to see him tipping the barrow's contents onto the compost heap.

'Fetch the fork, will you son?'

I jog back with the fork and see Dad burying something with his foot.

'What was it?'

'You don't want to know.'

'Not another one?'

'No,' he says taking the fork from me and stabbing it into the compost.

'Just these.'

He unearths two little sack cloth dolls, a single stitch for their eyes, mouth and nose, making them look more like evil cats than anything human.

'And the usual champagne bottles, candles, and feathers.'

'Feathers? From what?'

'I wonder?' he says, all sarcastic.

'Crow? Magpie?'

Dad shrugs and reburies the evil cats and I get my answer as I glimpse an oily black feathered head and beak.

I want to ask if he thinks that's where the blood on the curtains is from. But he's already wheeling the barrow back up the path.

My foot hovers over the mound.

'Ryan James,' he growls.

I tear myself away. After he dumps the barrow at the door, we go straight to the first floor master bedroom.

'I won't be long. Why don't you start on the two bathrooms. I've checked them already. They just need a wipe round,' he says, *Vanish* in one hand, closing the door with the other.

I put my ear to the door, listening to Dad grunting and cursing before shouting the familiar: 'Never again!'

A few minutes later, Dad emerges and we head to Room 10, a large double.

The stench of stale river water hits us as soon as he opens the door. It smells like the trout Uncle Tom sometimes brings when he visits.

'Jesus,' says Dad, looking down at the bed. 'It's soaked through. The mattress will be ruined; there's no way they're getting their deposit back.'

'What the hell were they doing?'

'Nelson said they were doing the dolphin thing this year but I thought he meant it figuratively.'

'Figuratively?'

'I didn't think he actually believed they could summon the spirit of an Amazonian dolphin and do it.'

'Do what?'

'You know. They do it,' he said nodding his head at the bed. 'The dolphin does the...business with the ladies.'

'A dolphin? That's disgusting!'

'It's not an actual dolphin. It's the spirit of a dolphin.'

'It's still disgusting.'

'This is disgusting,' says Dad sniffing around the bed like a dog.

He pulls back the soggy velvet bedcover to reveal a saturated mattress, sprouting patches of bright green algae fur.

I clamp my hand over my nose.

'You know I saw them outside last night.'

Dad looks up at me. 'Hope they didn't see you spying on them. That's in the contract. No prying, taking photos or asking questions.'

'I wasn't prying. I couldn't sleep. That women who always complains. She was dribbling -.'

'You saw the cleansing then,' interrupts Dad, scooping handfuls of algae into the bucket. 'I pay a fortune for a therapist, they pay a fortune for an annual spiritual cleanse.'

'If Mum knew what was going on...knew you were renting this place out to a voodoo society.'

'It's not voodoo. It's macumba.'

'I've Googled it, Dad. It's pretty much the same thing.'

'It's nothing like it,' says Dad, jabbing a slimy green forefinger at me. 'Now don't you dare say anything!'

'I wouldn't, not after last year. I wouldn't mind but I was the one who found it. What about the effect on me? I still can't get that image out of my head. It looked just like Squeaker.'

'Squeaker died when you were seven.'

'I was 11. He had the same sweep of hair and centre parting,' I say. 'Why do you think Mum was so upset? She'd hand-reared him.'

'Stop for a moment, Ryan and think. How could it have been Squeaker? He was a brindle. That one was ginger,' says Dad yanking back the sheets. 'Help me with these.'

I stomp to the other side of the bed and tug back the soggy sheets, remembering how I'd spotted its glassy eyes gazing up at me from underneath the piano stool as I sat on the sofa watching Coronation Street. In hindsight, I should have ignored it until Mum had left the room. But I couldn't help glancing at it. Wondering if it really was Squeaker back from his grave with a new hairdo? Or had a fox dug him up and Bernard, our cat, brought him in? When I looked closer I realised, of course, it couldn't be him. He'd been dead for four years. He'd be a skeleton, whereas this one looked very much in rude health before our guests had cut off its head.

Dad had managed to convince Mum the head belonged to an obese squirrel we'd seen Bernard eyeing up as it struggled to climb the willow tree. However, he couldn't quite so easily explain how Bernard had managed to get hold of the bloody pile of entrails she'd found under one of the beds. Dad shoves the mattress up against the wall.

'We'll leave it overnight. Say one of the guests spilled some tea and then you came along and accidently knocked a bucket of water all over it.'

'Why me? Why can't you -,' I begin to say as the phone in reception rings.

'Get that, will you. It's probably your Mum, letting us know she's about to leave.'

'But -?'

'It's okay, don't worry. I'll finish off up here,' says Dad, patting the mattress with a towel.

I run down the stairs and throw myself at the phone.

'Hello, Mum?'

A familiar voice greets me.

I place my hand over the receiver and shout up the stairs.

'Dad!'

He's already half way down and when he's at the bottom, I whisper: 'Are you going to tell him where he can stick his AGM?'

Dad nods and takes the receiver before shooing me back upstairs. I linger halfway up, out of sight but still in earshot.

'Hello.! Yes, quite a bit. A new mattress, new curtains and possibly a new carpet in Room 10. We're looking at about £2,000 over the deposit.'

I strain my ears waiting for Dad to tell them.

'That's very generous. Yes, you can pay it directly into the account,' he says.

I bristle at Dad doing his fake 'I'm such a great host' laugh.

'No worries. Er, same time next year, you say? Well, I'm not sure if we're already booked. Dover Taxis have been on the phone about a dinner and dance. ...Oh...really? That's very tempting but I'm not sure I can cancel. They've already paid a hefty deposit. Let me just see what I can do.'

I hear the diary pages rustling and cross my fingers tightly. 'Ah, yes, that's all booked for you...And you, Nelson. De nada!'

First published in Bridge House's Crackers anthology.

Pyramid

'Oh, and did I mention a pyramid has turned up in the field next door?' says Mum.

'Mmm, I know,' I begin to say before the words register. 'Sorry, what did you say?'

'I drew back the curtains Tuesday morning and there it was. Nearly covers the whole field.'

'Really, Mum? A pyramid?' I say, rolling my eyes. 'Egyptian or Central American?'

'You're the one with the archaeology degree. You'll have to come and see it.'

I think of the four-hour drive to see this so-called pyramid, only to be faced with a field full of hay bales.

'It's just the way they've stacked the hay. Remember the Lego man Bob made when we were kids?'

'Bob's knees won't let him do that anymore.'

'Maybe it's those crop circle artists then... a statement haystack.'

'No, Bob would know about it. Anyway, why do you keep going on about haystacks? It's made of str -.'

'Straw bales, hay bales! Pretty much the same thing,' I interrupt.

'Tell that to the cows. Anyway, if you'd let me finish, it's made of *stone*. It's very impressive.'

'Really,' I say, trying to quell the rising irritation in my voice. 'So how come it's not been on the news?'

'Ah, no Bob's trying to keep it hush-hush. Doesn't want people trampling over the fields and scaring the cows. He's covering it up in black plastic.'

'Just like the hay bales,' I mutter.

'What did you say?'

'Nothing.'

* * *

Two days later, I pick up my sister from Euston Station and we head to Mum's.

'I'm officially worried. We need to get her assessed for dementia. She's been getting this way for a while. Remember Christmas?' says Kylie.

'How could I forget.'

'It was so embarrassing her asking Elaine if Philip Schofield could see into her sitting room too,' says Kylie as we turn off the motorway. 'Imagine if she'd come out with that rubbish when she was teaching. Apparently, he was commenting on her new slippers.'

'At least he wasn't telling her to kill people.'

'Or maybe he was,' smiles Kylie. 'And she's waiting for us to arrive.'

'Don't. I spoke to my friend, the care home manager. She said go along with whatever she says as long as it's harmless. Apparently, they get angry if you contradict them,' I say.

'What's new?'

'A pyramid though?'

'She probably saw a documentary about *The Lost Pyramids of Wackamackalacka* and then saw a load of bales out of the window,' says Kylie.

'Well, we'll find out in a minute,' I say, turning into a familiar windy road snaking its way up the hill into the village.

Henchmen cows look up either side of the road as if letting us know they've got their eyes on us out of towners. We glance across at three identical executive houses, each with a shiny four-wheel drive posing outside, all traces of the working men's club and our higgledy-piggledy Victorian school gone. Our playing field of daisies and eternal summer days are now gardens decorated with barbecues, patios, trampolines the size of a modest family home and giant climbing frame-swing-slide extravaganzas.

'Can you imagine the boast offs they have at their parties?'

'I don't recognise this area anymore,' I say, swallowing the urge to cry.

'You sound like Mum.'

'Well, it's true,' I say, my voice strangely squeaky.

I wait for Kylie to mimic me but she murmurs her agreement instead. We turn at the church, the gravestones still hanging on for dear life, threatening to topple onto the road. Opposite lies the Hamilton's old house. Even though I know they're long gone, I still expect to see garish orange curtains hanging in the windows. The white wooden shutters feel like a kick to my stomach.

'Pyramid or hay bales?' asks Kylie.

'On the balance of probability, I think I'm going to have to go with hay bales.'

We round the bend and come to the stretch before Mum's house, more cows staring us down. Both of us lean forward as if the act will give us telescopic powers. However, we don't need them. In the twilight, we see the pyramid, its black plastic sides flapping in the wind like an obese beast trying and failing to take flight.

* * *

'They wouldn't have done that if Dad was still around. They're taking advantage,' I say, leaning down to give Mum a hug.

'The Mexicans?'

Me and Kylie stifle our smiles.

'No, Bob and the landowner,' I say.

'It's got nothing to do with them. It's those Mayans. Go and see for yourself,' she says, opening the door and peering into the twilight.

'It's a little dark but why not,' I say, deciding to call Mum's bluff. 'Coming?'

'Maybe it's best to leave it until morning. They're still a bit upset about Bob covering it up,' Mum says, quickly shutting the door.

'It's too cold to be poking a load of hay bales anyway,' says Kylie, plonking our overnight bags in the hallway.

'I wish you'd stop going on about hay bales,' Mum says, as we follow her into the kitchen and I stick the kettle on.

'Apparently, it was off course. Meant to land in that park next to the Pitt Rivers Museum but the navigation was slightly off.'

'Oh, yeah. I was thinking of getting one to Spain this year,' says Kylie.

'There's no need for sarcasm, young lady. I'm as much in the dark as you are. Maybe your sister can shed some light on it.'

'I studied ancient history of the Near East, Mum,' I say, reaching into the cupboard for the teabags.

'I thought you knew everything about pyramids. I've told them you're an expert.'

'Er, no, Mum,' I say turning round to see her face crumpling in disappointment. 'Told who?'

'But you went to Mexico on that study trip.'

'I went to Turkey on a study trip. I went to Mexico on holiday about ten years ago.'

'She went to Mexico for two weeks and therefore's an expert on everything Mayan,' says Kylie, rolling her eyes to the ceiling.

Mum catches her and I see her wince. I quickly try and recall some facts.

'I think there was a big mystery about the Mayans because they all seemed to disappear at the end of the 9th century,' I say. 'No one's sure what happened to them. They either died from a plague or famine. Some of the wackier theories say the pyramids were landing areas for spaceships.'

Kylie lets out a massive snort-laugh as she fetches the tray.

'Laugh all you like. The chap in charge said they'd seen Oxford on Google Earth and took a fancy to it. I'll get the milk for you,' says Mum, walking towards the fridge.

'Google Earth?' we both say, our mouths dropping open.

'Something to do with a tourist's lost mobile. That's where they saw images of Oxford and thought it looked impressive. People riding bikes.'

'The flying pyramid pilot is impressed by people riding bikes?' says Kylie.

'No, silly, not just the bikes but people wearing glasses and tweeds. It's a look, he says, they don't have much of in Mexico. Got fed up with all the drug dealing and killings, apparently. It was putting visitors right off. Anyway, enough about the pyramid. Come into the sitting room and you can see what I mean about those bloody TV presenters.'

'Should we mention a visit to the doctor?' Kylie whispers as we follow Mum.

I shake my head. 'Let's wait until we make an appointment, then we'll sell it to her as an over 80s health check.'

* * *

The next morning I wonder why it's still dark outside until I draw the curtains, and see the wall of bales. Kylie comes in with a cup of tea shortly afterwards, half her face lined like contours on a mountainside.

'Mum was clatter-banging big time last night, talking to herself,' says Kylie, yawning.

'Poor Mum. Apparently, they have trouble sleeping and wander around in the night,' I say.

'I went downstairs and she said it was the 'Mexican chap' wanting to borrow some clothes because he was cold,' says Kylie.

'Oh God, the sooner we make that appointment, the better,' I say as we hear the steady rhythm of Mum's walking stick hitting the stairs.

A few moments later, she pokes her head around the door.

'You never guess what I've just heard on the radio?'

'A Mexican pyramid's been reported missing?' Kylie suggests.

'Oh, you heard. That lady archaeologist was so upset. She travelled there with her team to excavate it and it'd vanished. She's demanded the Mexican government investigate. Apparently, they've been after demolishing it for years to build a road,' she says, walking towards the window. 'Looks like a nice kind of day.'

'If you could see it,' says Kylie.

'You can kind of see the light reflected on the bales.'

Mum shoots me a look before turning away as we hear a tractor growling up the drive.

'That'll be Bob now with the Mexican chap. How do I look, girls?' she says teasing her grey curls as she leaves the room.

'Fine,' we both say, looking at each other in horror.

'You don't think?' says Kylie.

I hold my hand out like a big fat full stop.

* * *

We get dressed and hurry into the farmyard to see a man wearing grey jogging pants and a matching sweatshirt.

'Dad?' we both say.

Of course, we know it's not him. He's been dead for five years. And as we get closer, I realise the tracksuit swamps the dark-skinned stranger.

'There you are,' says Mum, waving.

'Mexican my arse,' says Kylie. 'He's Eastern European.'

The stranger turns to face us and slowly bows down from his waist like we're royalty.

'Babak, these are my daughters,' says Mum.

'Oh, he has a name now, unlike us,' I say.

He holds out a smart phone to Mum who slowly types something in before looking up.

'This Mayan translator app is marvellous,' she says, going back to typing.

Me and Kylie pull a face at one another.

She shows the screen to Babak who smiles, revealing teeth like stumpy sticks of chalk. He types something in reply. Mum giggles, then blushes.

'He says, 'don't you mean your sisters'!' Mum twitters.

'The creep,' mutters Kylie.

Babak bows from the waist again.

'Is he helping Bob on the farm?' I ask, taking sneaky glances at his greasy greying hair as he types something in the phone.

'I don't think so,' says Mum, frowning.

'He's so obviously looking for farm work,' says Kylie.

'Who is?' says Mum, glancing behind her.

'The stranger in your dead husband's clothing,' says Kylie, her lip curling.

But Mum isn't listening. She's staring at the mobile, her head nearly touching Babak's as he types away. She looks up.

'He says, would you like a tour of the pyramid?'

'This is ridiculous,' I mutter.

'Why not?' says Kylie, linking her arm through mine.

Mum and Babak walk off, stopping every now and then to type something into the phone, giggling like teenagers.

'Just humour her. Once she knows they're just a stack of hay bales, she'll see this phoney Mayan for the chancer he really is,' says Kylie.

I watch Babak open the gate to the field and notice Mum's missing something.

'She always has her stick, especially on bumpy ground,' I say, incredulous.

'Obviously the Mayan has miraculous powers.'

'Come on slow coaches! We'll be round the other side,' Mum calls as she disappears behind the bales.

A few minutes later, we turn the corner to see Babak crouching down, his hand hovering over the black plastic.

'Ready?' says Mum.

We nod, trying to keep the smirks off our faces. Mum, in turn, nods her head at Babak and he yanks back the plastic to reveal a smooth stone entrance lit inside by a single flaming torch, not one stalk of hay in sight.

Long listed for the Colm Tóibín International Short Story Award 2017.

Shadow Legs

Gracie often admired her shadow self on sunny days, marvelling at how impossibly long and thin her legs were. Almost the length of a giraffe's, she'd think to herself.

She liked to imagine what it would feel like to own them, to parade up and down Sunny Sands on those fine pins. To feel the warmth of admiring glances and the coldness of envious stares. She visualised just how they'd feel to walk on; light and delicate but strong and flexible.

So, when her shadow sidles up to her one day, and asks if she'd like to do a leg swap, how could she resist?

* * *

She hits the High Street straight away. Tries on all the skinny jeans she can find. Whoops in delight as she squeezes her shadow legs into a size 8 in every store, three sizes smaller than normal. And best of all, she doesn't have to roll up a single pair. She even has to complain in one shop because the jeans stop short of her ankles. But she can live with not being able to shop there. With her legs eleven, she realises she's going to have to rethink her usual retail habits and promises herself a visit to a more upmarket shopping centre. She skips towards home, only too aware of the gawps of fellow shoppers, many of whom, she is delighted to see, include several girls from the year above.

It's Saturday tomorrow, she realises with relish. She's meeting her best friend, Freya, at Sunny Sands and can't wait. Never again would she have to hide under her towel to take her clothes off, or undress on the shoreline so she could run straight into the sea. She'd pose next the arches. Even better the steps, where everyone worth knowing gathered. She'd snigger at the sunbathers toasting their doughy flesh as they wallowed like pigs among their discarded lager cans, plastic bags and Poundland snacks. Then, she'd saunter down to the sea, where she'd make a great display of kicking at the waves. She felt like she may spontaneously start dancing, but decided that may be a bit over the top, a bit like showing off. She'd have to try and be a bit humble about her great legs, especially as they were now longer and thinner than Freya.

No-one had longer or thinner legs than Freya's.

To be honest, she wasn't sure how Freya would take it. You see, there was an unwritten rule between them whereby Gracie had the best nose and mouth and Freya, the best legs. It was a delicate balance of power, dictated by playground peers since primary school.

But now the nose/mouth versus legs power axis had shifted, she didn't know whether Freya would still want to be friends with her.

In fact, did she even want to be friends with Freya? Did she even need Freya, she wonders as she spots Charisma and Channel coming up the Old High Street, tucking into a bag of chips.

'Wow, you look amazing,' says Charisma.

'Almost like you've been super-stretched,' says Channel, staring at her legs.

Gracie blushes under their gaze, unsure how to deal with this new found attention from the most popular girls at school.

'I mean is it like...like...one of those new celebrity treatments? The stretching rack?' she asks.

An image from a documentary of common medieval tortures pops into Gracie's head.

'No!'

'Big Bang then?' asks Channel.

For a split second Gracie is completely thrown. She wonders if Channel wants her to say something meaningful about the beginning of the universe. What with Stephen Hawking dying recently, was theoretical physics the new thing to be in to?

'The Big Bang. The new celeb diet?' she explains.

Of course, thinks Gracie. Charisma and Channel are always on a diet, even when they're consuming chips.

Gracie wonders whether to come clean and tell them the truth. But then everyone will have long, skinny legs and she's wanted them for so long. It didn't seem fair that everyone else should have a pair.

'You know? Eat nothing bigger than an at-om,' says Charisma.

'My aunt tried it and had to be hospitalised after two weeks,' adds Channel.

'5-2 diet?' asks Charisma, looking her up and down.

Gracie nods, vaguely recognising the diet as one of many she's read about.

'It's worked wonders for you,' says Channel, a chip poised in her hand as she stares at Gracie's legs and shakes her head in awe.

'We're going to the beach tomorrow if you want to come?' says Charisma.

'I'm meeting Freya.'

The two look at each other and roll their eyes.

'Low tide at midday. We'll be in the fourth arch along. Don't bring Freya,' says Channel.

* * *

Gracie's mum gives her a double-take as she leaves the house.

'You've grown again. In a day?'

'I haven't seen you for three days, Mum.'

'Still. You'll be through the roof before long.'

Gracie wonders if she should tell her the truth. Find out if it's okay to swap body parts with your shadow but her mum's already half way out of the door.

'Tea's in the oven. Dad'll be home at 9pm. If you need any-thing, go next door. And no more growing. Love you,' she calls as she slams the door.

Gracie stares at the door's peeling blue paint, trying to recall if she's ever overheard her parents, or any friends talking about shadows asking to swap. She didn't remember seeing any 'shadow stranger danger' public health warning films. She certainly didn't learn about it in biology. It's got to be safe, she reasons.

But just in case, she Googles it. She scans down pages and pages of articles written by male fitness gurus screaming *'From fat to fit in 9 days'* and there's even one about *'Getting rid of women's ugly strawberry legs'*. Gracie's mouth hangs open. The day was indeed turning very strange. It's on a par, she thinks, with the day she came across a video about the Milkmen, a whole movement of men breast feeding babies. As she imagines her torso attached to two giant juicy strawberries, her leg swapping issues begin to pale into insignificance. How would you stop strawberry lovers taking a bite out of your legs? Or was the ugly strawberry reference yet another shape to shame women with? Eventually her mind calms as she reads it's a reference to little pin pricks of red appearing after shaving your legs. Gracie looks down at her shadow legs and smiles. They're as smooth and hairless as the Hollywood.

She decides then she must have made it happen, just like all those positive thinking quotes littering social media. You could literally think yourself a new pair of legs. There wasn't a day she hadn't bemoaned the uncomfortable feeling of fat rubbing between the top of her thighs, the cellulite that'd seemingly appeared overnight, the mean remarks during games about her resembling a weightlifter. Every time she inadvertently caught a glimpse of her legs in the mirror, she'd felt a little piece of herself shrivel inside. They didn't belong to her.

Now she'd got what she wanted, should she share this new-found knowledge with the world? Become an influencer, amassing millions of fans? Apply it to other areas of her life? Grade 9s in her GSCEs? Lottery win for mum and dad? World peace?

* * *

Nightmares plague Gracie that night. She dreams she wakes in the morning to find nothing but her crinkled sheet where her legs should be. Only when she pulls herself across the bed to the window and opens her curtains, the sunlight flooding into her bedroom, do her new legs reappear. She spends all morning checking in every mirror that her legs remain attached to her body. And when she steps out into the sunshine, she breathes a big sigh of relief; her usual shadow is waiting for her, lolling across the driveway.

Gracie walks to the steps leading to Sunny Sands, trying to ignore the dozens of messages from Freya, as well as the odd sensation of lightness in her legs. She turns off her phone and distracts herself from the floaty feeling by looking across to the beach below. Hundreds of people have already marked out their territory, and are busy building elaborate sandcastles, sunbathing or splashing about in the gentle waves. Families weighted down with huge beach bags, overflowing with towels, buckets and spades, pass by on their way home for lunch. She feels something twist inside her as she fondly remembers doing the same, not so long ago, when life was so much simpler and she wasn't expected to be anything but a child.

She climbs down the steps, aware of how her cotton trousers no longer flap around her legs but almost invade them. How stupidly weightless her legs feel as if they may dissolve at any moment. They're certainly not the lithe, supple limbs she'd imagined and is pleased she wore trainers and not flip-flops, otherwise her legs were in danger of floating off across the Channel. And there's something else troubling Gracie. She can see now that her shadow legs cast a much lighter shadow compared to her body. Like someone got fed up with shading in her legs and went off to do something more interesting. And she wonders for the first time when she can get her real legs back.

'Bagged the best spot,' says Channel when Gracie arrives.

Gracie holds her bag to her chest as if the very act will make her feel more grounded. She tries to think of an excuse to leave. She'll call Freya. Tell her everything.

But Charisma grabs her bag and dumps it into the gloomy arch.

'Come on then,' says Channel, stripping off to her sparkly orange bikini. 'We've been waiting, so we can all go in together. Give the lard-arses something to aspire to.'

Gracie pulls down her leggings, pleased to be distracted by someone doing acrobatics near the shoreline. Whoever it is, they've drawn quite a crowd of small children with their cart wheeling and flipping in and out of the waves. There's something mesmerising about the fluid movement of the legs, the sheer energy of the display and even the legs themselves. They're muscular and athletic and strangely familiar. She squints into the sun to get a better look, thinking perhaps it's someone from her gymnastics class from a couple of years ago. They're spinning through the waves so quickly they look like a cartoon blur, almost like they don't have a body. And when they slow and resurface from the sea, she stumbles back into the wall of the arch, realising the legs aren't actually attached to a body because they're her legs.

'Where...?' says Channel, who is now backing away from her, pointing at where Gracie's legs should be.

When Gracie glances down, she sees her shadow legs have merged with the shade to make it look as though her torso is hanging over her beach towel.

She looks up to see her magnificent legs hurtling towards her, coming back to her at last; somersaulting through the gaps between sunbathers, kicking sand into faces and over picnics. A little blonde toddler squeals in delight, his mother sweeps him up in her arms as the legs whirl by. Other people are screaming, scrambling to their feet and fleeing up the steps, leaving their belongings scattered over the beach. And Gracie feels nauseous as she remembers something she'd forgotten from her dream; the sensation of being tricked by her shadow.

She hover-sprints towards her legs, catching up with them near to the rock pools and tackles them to the ground, trying several times to sit atop them and force them back into position. But they're too slippery, and far too powerful. They wriggle free from beneath her and leap into the sea, vanishing as her shadow head emerges through a wave, laughing.

'You can't catch me!'

First published in To Hull and Back 2018 Short Story Short List Anthology.

Homecoming Queen

The world is out of sorts today. The seagulls are going squawking-crazy. They keep flocking on the harbour arm before swooping over the town's most popular beach, Sunny Sands, and starting the whole business again.

The tide is all wrong too. It's tsunami far out, like a monster has sucked the sea away. Low tide usually stretches to the beginning of the harbour arm. Today, it's doubled its distance to the lighthouse. But maybe it's my memory playing tricks on me? Perhaps 20 years of city living has changed my perception around distances and it's always been that far out. I swear not, though, and start panicking. Perhaps that's why no one's here? There's a tsunami coming and they've all fled inland. There's no one to warn me. Except Cally, though she's vanished too.

And then there's the sky. It looks like it's auditioning for one of those Scandinavian misery-fest dramas. The sea and sky an interchangeable grey with the faintest tinge of yellow. I scrunch my eyes shut and open them. It makes no difference. The light is all wrong. I wonder if it's the start of a migraine. I have a hangover headache, yes. Not the tight iron band squeeze of a migraine.

I tell myself to trust my judgement. I was born and raised here for 16 years. The light always had an otherworldly feel to it, gifting the landscape more colour and depth than anywhere else I've ever visited. But today it's like the air is full of dust. It feels unclean and too still, almost like looking through stale vase water. I take off my glasses, thinking they're grimy, misted up or both. But when I wipe them on the hem of my dress, there's no change, except it's grown darker. The sun, wherever it is, has had enough and is off to bed, leaving behind a dirty dusk protest.

I check my mobile to see if I have a signal yet. It's still infuriatingly intermittent. One moment, it's fine. The next, you're cut off, or receive a text from your provider welcoming you to France. I decide to walk back towards the harbour arm where we spent last night, drinking rhubarb cider and reminiscing. I was so surprised to hear from Cally. We'd been best friends at secondary school. Even became blood sisters, an innocent ritual that took place on top of a huge slug of a rock known affectionately as Old Herbert on Sunny Sands. He was our very own Jabba the Hut, us his Princess Leias voluntarily spilling our blood over his gruesome head. There was even a stupid legend saying Old Herbert came alive every 100 years to demand one of the town's own. A payback for all the sea creatures the fishermen harvest from his territory.

One day, our history teacher caught us comparing our cuts in class and sent us to talk to the counsellor about our supposed self-esteem issues. Soon after, Dad was posted to Germany. We wrote letters for a while but then lost touch. I went to university and Cally stayed at home working for her father and brothers, all fishermen.

Fifteen years later, she contacted me out of the blue, via Twitter. Recognised my picture, apparently. Haven't changed at all, she lied. Come for the Bank Holiday weekend. You wouldn't recognise the town now. The ferries have gone but we have an art festival every three years. The whole town's full of weird sculptures. And it's the Harvest Sea Festival. You were crowned the Sea Queen for three years running for goodness sake! You've got to come. It's always a good laugh.

And it was. We spent Saturday watching her brothers win the trawler race and the Bishop blessing the fisheries, in between visiting our old haunts. We ended up at the newly refurbished harbour arm with her extended family. They treated me like a long lost daughter, refusing to let me buy a single drink, helping me to drown my sorrows about my recent break up. I can't even remember getting back to Cally's. I must have passed out and didn't wake up until 4pm. Cally was nowhere to be seen. I assumed she'd popped to the shops. But by 6pm and after several dozen calls to her switched off mobile, I gave up waiting. When I left her flat, near the harbour, everything was eerily quiet for a Sunday evening. No cars. No day trippers. No dog walkers. No scrounging cats. Only seagulls fussing.

I take my phone from my pocket and wince. The plaster on my wrist is hanging off and the cut is oozing. Stupid of me, I know. For old time's sake, said Cally, as we drunkenly clambered onto Old Herbert's mollusc-covered head and she passed me the knife. It felt wrong. It'd always felt wrong to be honest but Cally was always so persuasive.

I feel like I'm going to throw up and lean against a seaweedy wall to let the nausea pass. I need to eat and glance across at the harbour car park, relieved to see lines and lines of cars. I can just make out people on the arm, like stickmen, either strolling along, or sitting at picnic tables. I feel my body relax, remembering Cally saying how it's the place to be at weekends, to the extent where the rest of the town is deserted. My mobile buzzes in my pocket. A message at last.

How's your head? Thought I'd let you sleep. Come down to the champagne bar. Hair of the dog!

I text to say I'm on my way, my fingers feeling as slow to respond as my brain. I vaguely recall a conversation last night, snippets of it now drifting away like a dream; Cally telling me a friend, or was it one of her father's friends, had invited her to lunch at the champagne bar in the old lighthouse.

I half crawl up the stairs to the iron railway bridge which spans the sea and leads to the old harbour station on the arm. Its rails have been ripped up and replaced with neat tarmac paths and gravelly flower beds. Half a dozen seagulls, sitting on benches, eye me up for chips and ice cream. Up ahead, two cormorants, watch my progress from the arm's entrance gates. One of them swoops down and lands in front of me, spreading its raggedy wings as if trying to bar my way. I step towards it and it flies back to its mate.

Once through the gates, the wind picks up, its icy little fingers teasing the back of my neck. I pull my flimsy cotton jacket around me, and shiver, remembering how cold it was last night when the sun went down.

I glance back at Sunny Sands. From this new perspective, it looks like Old Herbert has crept several hundred yards closer and I think the tide must be coming in now. But when I look out to sea, I can't work out what's going on because the tide is still out as far as the lighthouse. And when I look back along the harbour arm, it's deserted. I assume everyone has been driven inside by the wind and push on to the former train station's waiting rooms, abandoned in my day, but now tastefully renovated and converted into restaurants and cocktail bars.

I make my way along the corridor, listening out for signs of life but all I hear are my own footsteps and my stomach rumbling at the thought of the fish and chips I ate last night; the beer-battered cod was to die for. I tell my stomach it will get food soon and glance hopefully through each restaurant window. They're all closed, though the tables are covered with crackers, party poppers and balloons, set up for a celebration of some sort.

I carry on to the champagne bar to find tables and chairs outside deserted, the door locked, lights off. As I look through the little glass door panel, I hear something scuttling, a person running perhaps, and the sound of a chair being scraped across the floor. Bunting is dangling from the ceiling and dozens of sparkling champagne glasses sit atop the tables, one of which is wobbling slightly, setting the glasses tinkling. I glance around me, half expecting Cally and her family to jump out and shout 'surprise.'

'Cally?' I shout into the silence.

There's a sharp rap on the window behind me and I turn, smiling, thinking it's her or one of her brothers playing a trick on me. But there's no one there except a seagull, standing on the windowsill outside, looking so smart like it's washed and ironed its feathers for the imminent party inside. It taps the glass with its shiny beak several more times and flies off.

I glance around urgently, trying to work out where Cally is and where all the people I saw earlier have gone. Perhaps there was another exit I didn't know about, I think, spinning around trying to find it. But I feel so sick, I can't think straight and hurry back along the arm, listening to the waves hit the pebbly beach on the other side, making their shh sound. I want to tell them to shut up, there is no one to silence. But I wish there was because it's overbearing and if I had the energy I would run straight back to the train station and get the hell out of here. I glance across at the Channel, expecting to see flickering lights of cargo ships ploughing back and forth. But there are none. And when I look beyond, even France is hiding from me.

A yelping disturbs the quiet. I spot a large black dog on Sunny Sands. It's running in small circles. I squint, trying to work out what it's chasing and where its owner is. But as I get closer, I can see he's not playing. The dog is trying to escape its tether; one of Old Herbert's jagged teeth. The dog's desperate whimpering cuts through me like the wind and I clamber down a rusty ladder to the beach below.

In the twilight, it looks like Old Herbert has moved closer, almost like he's moving. And as I watch him crush the dog, I realise, I'm right. He is moving. Raising his ginormous head, Old Herbert's seaweed nostrils sniff the air and he slithers towards me, the sand beneath him slurping and sucking like there are more monsters lying beneath ready to burst out.

I glance back at the ladder, wondering if I can reach it in time, and as I do so, I catch sight of hundreds of people smiling down at me from the harbour arm. And when I look back, Old Herbert's slobbering jaws become the sky and cheering fills the silence.

First published in the Ritual issue, Here Comes Everyone. It's also at Folkestone Harbour Arm, Kent. If you ever visit, have a look out for the QR code to listen to a recording of the story.

Adventure Time in Brian May's Hair

It happened at St Tiggywinkles, a hedgehog sanctuary, just down the road from my mum's house. I'd gone hoping to meet my childhood hero; rock star, physicist and animal lover Brian May. He was officially opening the new spine regeneration wing where, as its name implied, scientists grew new spines for those hedgehogs unlucky enough to be the flat mate punch line.

I'd been queuing since 6am along with a load of Italian Queen fans, who, much to my annoyance, had arrived seconds before me. Just as I was parking, their coach had screeched to a halt and they all piled out, elbowing each other out of the way to be first in the queue. Subsequently, I found myself at number 63, in front of two ruddy-faced farmers, who turned up half an hour later, smelling of sour milk. They immediately unfurled two suspiciously new Queen flags and I wondered then, whether the flags were subterfuge: they were there to give Brian, the voice of the badger, a piece of their minds about the animals spreading TB.

I could tell the bonafide Queen fans. The Italians, for example, shivered in the mean March wind wearing various collectible Queen items, including my favourite, *It's a kind of Magic1986* tour T-shirt where the band are depicted like blue Mr Incredibles. There were even a couple of old timers showing off their 1980 *The Game* Tour T-shirts, Freddie all faded and deformed as he was stretched over their fat bellies. A few of the younger ones, who I very much doubted had ever seen Queen live, sported perms that would give Brian's locks a run for their money, while showing off dodgy tattoos of the band on their forearms, Freddie always singing his heart out in the forefront.

I glanced back at the farmer-types behind me. They were clearly amateurs with their red trousers and kaki body warmers. Me? I wore my Live Aid T-shirt, black *We Will Rock You* satin bomber jacket and rare official 1976 Queen scarf, all three drawing envious glances from the Italians.

I'd been a massive Queen fan ever since the Bohemian Rhapsody video burst into my life. The split screens are feeble stuff now, I know. But back in the 70s it was a dazzling display of what technology could do with a pop video. I'd never really warmed to the tune though, mostly because my older brother liked to wrap his school tie around my neck while singing: 'Mamma, just killed a boy, put a tie around his neck, pulled it tight and now he's dead'.

I'd suffered mild depression with the shock of Freddie dying so young, though he'd never been my favourite. Brian was always the one. He was impossibly clever, an amazing guitarist and by all accounts a very kind person. Since Live Aid, I'd never got the chance to see them perform again. So I couldn't believe my luck when I read in the local paper, he was visiting the area and I'd counted down the days, planning in detail what to wear and what time I'd leave the house.

At around 8am, a dark blue Mercedes with its windows blacked out, pulled up outside the iron gates of St Tiggywinkle's, expelling two fat-headed giants. As the gates opened, we surged forwards and the minders waved their arms at us as if we were a herd of TB-infected cattle.

'Hold your line or else you won't get to see Mr May,' shouted one of them, shoving an older, bespectacled Italian fan on his shoulder.

A few moments later, the minders allowed us into the driveway where we stood shuffling expectantly, hemmed in by VIP plastic tape.

'Mr May will have a tour and afterwards will answer any questions,' said one of the minders, who I suspected didn't appreciate his proximity to Brian.

The Italians took up most of the first row and as I'm pretty small I managed to squeeze myself into a corner next to a hedge. If I leant forward and twisted my head to the side, I had a great view. After about ten minutes, a short wiry man emerged from the spine regeneration wing, Mr Tiggywinkle himself.

'Welcome everyone,' he said. 'We're very pleased that Brian can take some time out of his music and astronomy to support our important work.'

We all clapped and cheered and there were smiles all round, even from the farmers who had managed to push their way to the front.

'Now Brian is happy to take questions about hedgehogs this morning but strictly no questions about Queen, Freddie Mercury or conspiracy theories.'

A disgruntled murmuring and tutting filled the air. I glanced back at the two farmers, shaking their heads at one another; genuine fans after all. Then I heard a collective gasp and looked back to see Brian had appeared in front of us just as the sun came out, his crowning glory lit up like a halo.

'So any questions?' asked Mr Tiggywinkle.

Several dozen tattooed arms punched the air.

Mr Tiggywinkle pointed to one of the few Italians without a perm.

'Why you like hedgehog?' the man asked.

'It's not that I like hedgehogs in particular, though I do like them of course. I like all animals,' said Brian.

'Did Freddie like hedgehog?' the fan asked,

One of the doorstop-necked minders stepped in.

'That's enough,' he said, bearing over the Italian fan.

'Take it-a easy!' said the fan, who stepped back and crashed into several other fans, all cursing loudly.

'Hey guys, no more Queen or Freddie questions or else I'll have to call it a day,' said Brian.

I placed my hand in the air. I thought my knees would give way as Brian walked towards me. But he stopped in front of the Italian next to me, who had taken off his jacket to reveal a tattoo of a naked Brian riding a tiger up his arm.

The fan was trembling so much I feared Brian may fall off the back of the shaky tiger any second and expose himself to me. I quickly averted my eyes.

'I can't remember question. I can't believe it's you.'

'It's okay, my friend,' said Brian, clearly unable to tear his eyes away from his naked self. 'Where are you from?'

'Milan. We travel all night.'

'Welcome to the UK!' said Brian. 'You have a question. About hedgehogs.'

I zoned out. I couldn't believe Brian was now standing right next to me. All that was separating me from my idol was a thin piece of plastic 'VIP' tape. If I leant forward a few inches, I could even reach out and touch his glorious curls tumbling over his shoulders. I closed my eyes as I breathed in the scent of his shampoo, an intoxicating geranium fragrance. When I opened them again, he'd turned his back to me to answer another inane question about hedgehogs and that's when it happened. I stuck my hand out to touch the bouncing locks of genius, at the same time as Brian flicked his head and before I knew it I was being swamped, then sucked into a vortex of greying curls that wrapped themselves tightly around my wrists and ankles. And the more I tried to struggle to free myself, the deeper into his thatch I went. Until I was trapped. A prisoner. I thought about pulling at it, screaming into his ear to let me go, but the thought of hurting Brian made me feel sick.

And then I realised there was nothing I could do. I'd just have to gently try and uncoil the knots while he answered more questions. I would surreptitiously jump down as and when the minders weren't looking.

I relaxed and listened to Brian answering a question about hedgehogs' favourite food and another about how many spines they have; insects and 8,000 if you were curious. Then one of the farmers started shouting: 'Brian May, you bloody badger lover! You're killing our cows!'

That's when Brian got bundled into the back of the Mercedes and I found myself squashed up against the leather seat, unable to breathe as we sped through the gates of St Tiggywinkle's and onto the motorway. I was just about to pass out, thinking that perhaps being suffocated by Brian's hair wasn't such a bad way to die after all, when the car slowed and turned.

'Thanks, mate. I'm bursting. Too much tea,' said Brian.

I felt myself being lifted into the air, paralysed by the thought I was going somewhere I did not want to visit with my hero. I twisted and turned, trying to writhe myself free, and with one almighty tug, I managed to unsnarl the hair coiled around my left ankle. Brian cursed and flicked his head violently.

'Are you all right Mr May?' asked one of his minders.

'My hair must have got stuck in the headrest,' he said, getting out of the car. 'Won't be a minute.'

I peeked out of the curls, watching the crowds in the service station staring, mouths agape as Brian hurried towards the toilets. I gave my wrists and right ankle one final tug, and dropped to the floor in time to see Brian give his hair another angry flick before disappearing into the men's.

I glanced around me. I'd landed on my back next to a Scoop the Digger ride. Bob and his faithful cat, Pilchard, and a little blonde boy stared down at me. I waved, got up, and brushed myself down, noticing large chunks of grey fur wrapped around my ankles and wrists. The little boy started crying. I ran to the exit, found a payphone and waited round the corner for my mum to fetch me.

* * *

At night, I like to take the hair out from underneath my pillow and stroke it. Sometimes, I fantasise about what if I'd stayed in his hair. What if Brian had held back on the tea drinking that day and he'd travelled straight home. I could have dropped out at night while he was in bed. And okay, he and Anita may have been a bit surprised, but hey, you never know they may have grown to like me. Love me even, as much as I love Brian.

Marlon Brando On My Breadboard

Marlon Brando appears on my breadboard on the very same day my sister dumps her cat on me.

When I go into the kitchen in the morning, there he is in his pre-supersized glory eyeing me from the sideboard. I pick him up and examine his beautiful face, etched in years of knife cuts, shaded in with some kind of oily spillage. I sniff, slightly recoiling at the smell of sardines, and he breaks into a smile. Marlon Brando is smiling at me. He can be as fishy as he likes.

The cat arrives late afternoon. I look into its cage to see a raggedy ball of dark brown fur, stained nicotine orange at the ends, like it has a 40 a day habit. It spins round to look at me with spaced out glassy green eyes. I take a step back as I clock its long white fangs resting on its fluffy chin.

'The teeth are off putting at first,' says my sister, Sarah as she rests the travel cage in the hallway. 'But the vet reassured us they're perfectly normal.'

Betsy, my daughter, kneels on the floor making strange kissy-kissy sounds, clearly unfazed by the vampire teeth. Sarah opens the cage. The cat sprints out and shoots up the stairs, leaving sweaty paw prints on the wooden steps. Besty scampers after it.

'He's under your bed, Mummy,' she shouts down.

'Best let him settle,' Sarah calls back.

* * *

Nick arrives home later that evening and disappears upstairs to change. After a few moments, we hear the sound of feet pounding down the stairs before he crashes into the kitchen. A smell follows, reminiscent of burnt toast. Mine and Betsy's noses twitch as we try to decipher the smell and where it's coming from, when a sudden waft makes us gag.

'There's a creature under the bed and it's done a shit on my gym kit bag,' he says.

It was more than he'd said to me all week.

* * *

Later, over dinner I say: 'I was going to tell you.'

Nick scrunches his eyes shut. 'Why the hell did you agree?'

'Betsy's been on about us getting a cat for ages... and he's already been re-homed twice. Sarah thought he'd been through enough already.'

'It's a cat.'

'In age, he's equivalent to a toddler.'

Nick stabs at a pasta shell.

'Why the hell did she get a bloody cat in the first place?' he asks, dropping his fork onto his plate.

It was a question we'd debated many times before on account of my sister's son suffering a terrible allergy to horse and dog hair. Nonetheless, she thought it a good idea to get him a cat for his tenth birthday. After the fourth visit to A&E where he was put on a nebuliser, the doctors told her to get rid of the cat.

'We don't know anything about it,' Nick says, kneading his temples.

'He's a cat. Not a paedophile,' I say.

'Our bedroom still stinks,' he says.

He gets up then, pushing his unfinished plate of pasta across the table before announcing: 'I'm sleeping in the spare bedroom.'

I scoop the pasta into the bin while I hold Marlon's gaze. He winks at me and mouths: 'Hey Stella!'

* * *

The next morning, a Saturday, Betsy changes the cat's name from Lestat to Raison.

'He's all brown and squishy,' she says as she holds him down on her bed and tries to tame his unruly fur with a doll's hairbrush.

I agree. He doesn't wear his fur well. He is super-furred which is absolutely fine on some cats but with Raison it sits badly on his body like an ill-fitting suit. It's as if he's stolen the fur from another cat and stuffed himself inside. You have an overwhelming urge to grab him and straighten it out. But no amount of brushing has any affect. The tufts of fur strain away from each other like opposing magnets.

Later, Betsy bullies me into buying expensive *Le Gourmet Chat* food with the photo of the fancy white cat on the front, wearing a matching diamante collar and tiara; a two-storey scratching post; a luxurious goose-feathered sleeping basket; an aromatherapy cat litter tray and a pink cat buggy with integrated drinks' holders which I hide beneath Betsy's bed.

Nick leans against the doorframe of the downstairs toilet, watching me and Betsy fill up the geranium-scented litter tray with grey rubble.

'Why can't we let him go outside?' he asks.

'He has to be kept in for two weeks so he knows this is his home,' says Betsy. 'Otherwise he'll get lost.'

'And?' he replies.

That evening, while watching *Britain's Got Talent,* we hear the squeak of the toilet roll holder in the downstairs bathroom spinning round and round. We look at one another, thinking one of two things: someone has broken into the house and is using our toilet, or we have a poltergeist.

We creep towards the toilet to see Raison standing on his hind legs, front paws manically paddling against the toilet roll until waves of *Smooth* champagne satin cover his stink. Betsy holds her nose with one hand and films Raison with her mobile in her other.

* * *

Cat Using Toilet Roll becomes an overnight You Tube sensation, clocking up two million views in a week.

When Betsy gets home from school, she dresses him in her teddies' clothes and parades him up and down the street in his cat pram. I watch from the bedroom window as she stops every couple of yards making a great show of extracting her chocolate milkshake out of its special holder, and sucking on the straw as

Raison's fans gaze at him through the little plastic window. Nick has to fight his way through the hoards of children waiting to touch the fur of fame.

The following week he comes home later and later.

But I don't care. In the evenings, when the school kids go home and I finish sweeping up their sweet wrappers, I stand Marlon up against the sofa cushion next to me and snuggle up to him.

* * *

We go to France for two weeks. I try to smuggle Marlon into my suitcase but Nick finds him during his third inventory check and shoves him up against the bread bin. As Nick hustles me out of the house, I hear Marlon shouting: 'Quo vadis, baby?'

On the tenth day, Betsy shakes me awake from an afternoon nap. She's crying. She pushes my phone into my face.

'Read it, Mummy, read it.'

I squint at the text and see it's from Roger, our neighbour, who is looking after Raison while we're away. I read it out loud.

'Raison has been missing for seven days. Getting worried.'

I hug Betsy tightly but inside I'm doing cartwheels. Out of the corner of my eye, I see Nick punching the air in joy and mouthing 'yes' before miming the action of a deranged driver running over an object and reversing over it.

'I'm sure Raison is fine,' he says, patting her back. "Let's go to Monkey Valley tomorrow and see the lemurs. That'll cheer you up.'

After Betsy cries herself to sleep, Nick pours me a large glass of wine.

'Seven days not looking good,' he says. 'Car, fox, poison?'

'I feel mean feeling happy,' I say. 'Maybe he's found an owner who appreciates him, who likes him even.'

'Do you think this is how people feel when they adopt children and they don't like them? They feel as they've been foisted on them?' says Nick.

'It's a cat, Nick. There's no comparison. You can't attribute the same emotion,' I say, wondering how Marlon's faring, his lovely face squashed up against the bread bin.

'I just hate the way Raison's taking over,' says Nick, lighting his cigarette and blowing a cloud of smoke in my face. 'The way he leaps up at doors and crashes them open as if he's some hot shot cowboy entering a saloon ready to take on all the bad boys.'

I take a gulp of wine before speaking.

'Yeah, I know. And then he just stands there and stares at you. It's almost like he's judging us.'

'Yes, you've hit the nail on the head,' says Nick. 'He is judging us. He's thinking, 'I'm a fucking *You Tube* sensation and you're a bunch of losers with your dead end jobs.' And he just turns round and walks out. He may as well stick two fingers up at us.'

'I wouldn't mind if he closed the door behind him,' I say.

'He does it on purpose. Let the lazy arses' arses get cold,' he says, refilling my glass so it's nearly overflowing. 'Have you heard from Rog?'

I take my phone from my pocket and smile.

'Nothing.'

Nick punches air again.

'By tomorrow it'll be eight days. And by the time we get back ten whole days. There's no way he's going to reappear. His nine lives are well and truly over.'

I watch the cigarette smoke vanish into the starry night and a thought comes.

'Oh, God! Maybe we should have got him insured?' I say.

Nick grinds the cigarette under foot.

'I tried. The insurance company said they'd only give us insurance to cover vet's fees. Nothing for sudden death, even if he is a fucking *You Tube* sensation.'

* * *

On the way to Monkey Valley the next morning, Betsy shrieks for us to stop.

I pull over. Nick jumps out and opens her door, thinking she's going to be sick.

But instead she sprints back along the road and prostrates herself in front of one of the many Christian shrines on the roadside.

'Jesus,' says Nick, slamming the passenger door.

'It's the Virgin Mary, actually,' I say.

* * *

When we arrive home, Raison is hanging around on top of the garage with a fox cub. Betsy leaps out of the car and the cub scuttles off into the back garden. Raison jumps down to greet her, meowing and rubbing himself against her legs.

'It's a miracle,' says Betsy, holding him up to the grey sky cat god.

I want to say, no Marlon Brandon appearing out of nowhere is a miracle, as I run to the kitchen, rescue Marlon from the sideboard and give him a kiss.

Betsy follows with Raison under arm, rummages around in her back pack, and there and then wrestles him into a pink bikini she bought at the market in Chinon. I watch her disappear into the garage. A few moments later, she re-emerges pushing the cat pram. Raison is peering through the plastic window looking strangely relaxed.

I place Marlon gently back on the sideboard and go to help Nick unpack the car.

'I thought foxes are meant to eat cats,' he says as he slams the suitcases onto the hallway floor.

'Probably gave up trying to get through the fur,' I say.

'Or maybe he was just about to tuck in,' says Nick, squaring up to me. 'If we'd stopped at that service station like I wanted to. If for once in your life you'd have just listened to me,' he adds, before turning and stomping back down the hallway to the front door.

The fox disappears, perhaps scared off by Raison's cross-dressing. But fleas hop up from Besty's bedding and red lumps emerge on Nick's hairy legs. I spend over £100 on flea powder, flea tablets, combs and a lecture from the vet on my poor cat-keeping skills. I spend a day spraying the house while Nick takes Betsy to his mum's for the weekend.

As I de-flea the house, I wish many bad things upon Raison: speeding cars; a rabid pack of dogs; a trail of poisoned cat biscuits laid down by a sociopathic cat hater; a gang of antisocial teen-agers with state-of-the-art airguns; a fall from a high branch into a deep water tank; a plane crashing into the town, with Raison being the only fatality. I share my fantasies with Marlon in the evening as I lay my head next to his.

'They are just fantasies, I know. I don't really wish for anything bad to happen to him,' I say.

'Ah, but this is no fantasy, no careless product of wild imagination,' he whispers.

* * *

On Monday morning, as I open the door to take Betsy to school for the first day of the autumn term, Raison rushes in. I see a flash of white around his mouth. When we walk out of the front door, we see little piles of bright white feathers or fur on the pavement and road.

Betsy picks up a handful. She rolls it between her fingers next to her left ear, then sniffs it like a cigar connoisseur before opening up her palm to allow a gust of wind to carry it away.

'It's definitely cat hair,' she says, watching it disappear. 'Do you think Raison has killed Le Gourmet Chat?'

'Not unless he's visiting from Paris,' I say.

But I begin to wonder if it's a message from the spirit world. Just as white feathers are sent as a sign you're being watched over by angels, the white fur is a warning. The cat god has been party to my thoughts too many times and is angered.

Later that night, I fall asleep on the sofa with Marlon nestled in my arms. I wake to hear screaming. It's dark. Footsteps thunder down the stairs. The light flashes on. Nick is standing in the doorway, his face flushed red.

'I got up to go to the toilet and he jumped me. The hairy bastard bit me!'

I blink in a Betsy shape pushing past Nick.

'You're so mean about him, Daddy,' she says, bleary-eyed. "He just wants to play.'

'What kind of monster has your sister unleashed upon us?' asks Nick, holding his hand up to the hall light.

We watch the blood drip crimson spots onto the beige carpet.

'The horror. The horror,' says Marlon, his voice muffled by a cushion.

* * *

For the rest of the week, Raison messes on Nick's bicycle seat, in his cycle helmet, his work shoes and trainers. He even takes over our bed at night, hissing and spitting at us if we try and move him on. And no matter how many times I vacuum, our duvet is constantly covered in a thick layer of fur and tiny bits of dirt.

Nick threatens to pack his bags. Instead, he moves into the spare room where he spends his evenings on the computer. I move Marlon onto the sofa bed with me, downstairs in the lounge. When I go to brush my teeth and hear Nick snoring, I hack into his email account.

'I knew it!' I say.

I read him the emails Nick has been sending *Smooth* toilet roll behind my back. The last one says: *I am happy to accept a five figure one-off cash payment for Raison's services.*

'Hey, you wanna hear my philosophy of life?' Marlon asks. 'Do it to him before he does it to you.'

I quickly write a reply and cc myself into the email.

I have been called away to work in a remote area of China and won't be contactable for the next four weeks. Please send your reply to my wife, Stella, who will be negotiating on behalf of Raison.

Marlon reads the email three times, then nods his approval. I send it and delete it.

In the morning, after Besty has gone to school, we wait three hours for Raison to take a dump and film it. Afterwards, I look up *Le Gourmet Chat's* head of marketing and fire off an email offering Raison's services and attach the film. Two days later, I get a reply from *Le Gourmet Chat's* director of marketing. I read it out to Marlon.

Thank you so much for exclusively showing us the video of Raison briefly turning to acknowledge the camera as he goes about his business. We're very keen to use the footage exclusively and would ask you not to post it on You Tube. We're looking forward to making Raison the new poster boy of our latest French cuisine menus, aimed at sophisticated cats and their owners. Please get in touch as soon as possible to discuss payment.

'One of them is going to make you an offer you can't refuse,' Marlon says.

* * *

The following week, Nick slips on a freshly regurgitated fur ball and crashes headfirst into the banister. Both his eyes swell black and blue. He packs his bags and leaves. I clear up the fur ball and ring the *Le Gourmet Chat* people, telling them about the *Smooth* toilet roll people. Straight afterwards, I ring the

Smooth toilet roll people and tell them about the *Le Gourmet Chat* people.

Smooth toilet roll pulls out as the bidding war reaches six figures.

When I tell Marlon, he closes his eyes and smiles.

'I've said it many times before and I'll say it again: never confuse the size of your pay check with the size of your talent.'

First published Funny Pearls.

The Dogs of Kavala

The dogs have it all sewn up in Kavala. On our first night, we have a pack of them trailing us; a boss-eyed Alsatian, a wannabe Shirley Temple mongrel, a collie whose job is to bark at white cars, and a thickly furred, cinnamon-coloured bear of a dog with an oversized cartoon-like tongue.

They follow us everywhere. Up the narrow streets as we browse the sardine-themed souvenir shops, or along the seafront, past the fishermen untangling their nets and hanging out their washing in the rigging. Sometimes they jog in front like security guards, checking if it's safe up ahead, or if a car approaches, one of them plants themselves in the middle of the road to let everyone know who is top dog. The locals are especially tolerant about the impromptu road blocks. They don't beep or shout. Instead, they sit in their cars like they have all the time in the world, or inch forward, careful not to harm a hair on the dogs' well-fed bodies.

By midnight, we're tired of being stalked by them, though perhaps stalking is the wrong word. It's more like they're keeping a respectful distance. Not close enough to be a pest and complain about, but near enough to keep an eye on us, a little like an overzealous neighbourhood watch association.

* * *

The next morning, as we leave the hotel, we clock the dog with the meaty tongue lying on the hotel's welcome mat. We exit through the spinning doors, hurry past and head towards the gigantic aqueduct stretching over the town. Two minutes later, he's jogging behind us.

'Just try to ignore him,' says Karly as we head up a cobbled street to the castle.

'But what the hell does it want?'

'It could be a coincidence.'

'Let's find out,' I say, stopping dead in my tracks.

The dog strolls ahead, oblivious.

'See,' says Karly.

She speaks too soon though. The dog turns and trots back down the hill, stopping a metre or so away.

We walk on a few paces to trick the dog into thinking we're carrying on up the hill and he strolls ahead. I check no-one is behind us, and yank Karly back. Within a minute, there's a comfortable distance opening up between us and the dog. We dart into a shop selling dozens of bunches of loofas and every imaginable pottery object decorated with sardines. A teenage boy sits behind the counter texting. We pretend to admire some shiny blue bowls, speculating on whether the dog has noticed we're no longer behind him and on the count of three, turn and scream; the dog is staring at us through the window, its tongue hanging to one side of its yellow fangs, its breath fogging up the glass. The teenager smirks and dips down. I'm worried he's reaching for some kind of dog-chasing weapon and I'm just about to tell him, it's okay, we're not really scared, when he re-appears holding a big bag of dog biscuits. He pours a generous heap into a large bowl next to the counter and places it on the pavement outside.

'Let's get out of here,' I say.

We slip past the dog, its snout busy chasing bone-shaped biscuits around the bowl, and jog up the hill, until we turn a corner, where we rest for a few moments. I sneak a look down the hill, relieved to see the coast is dog-clear and we continue our journey to the castle, past private houses, all crumbling along with the country's economy. We stop to admire the Imaret, an opulent Ottoman mansion where Muhammed Ali, the founder of modern Egypt, was born. It's now an obscenely expensive spa hotel and we laugh at the pricelist which is in such tiny print you almost need a magnifying glass to read it. I wonder how they can keep going as there's a dearth of tourists, despite it being the beginning of the season. It's a fact our airport taxi driver blames on the migrant crisis, though we've yet to come across any haunted-eyed Eritreans, Afghans or Syrians like the teenagers I teach English to back in Kent. In fact, we've yet to see any refugees in the town and I wonder if they've moved onto wealthier cities or even other countries.

When we reach the ramp up to the castle and round the corner to the entrance, we both start; our dog is lying in the shade beside the ticket booth, its tongue glistening in the sun like a giant slice of ham.

'What the hell!' says Karly.

'It could be a different one?' I suggest.

'There's no way two dogs in the same town could have the same freakish tongue. How on earth did it get here?'

The dog sits up but not to greet us. Shouting is coming from within the castle grounds. It's followed by the sound of glass, or pottery smashing.

'Maybe a wedding?' says Karly.

The dog stands. Its ears prick forward and nose twitches as if sniffing out trouble and he cautiously enters the castle grounds to investigate. We expect the ticket lady to jump out of her booth and join him, or at the very least, to shoo the dog away. But she seems unperturbed by both events, and instead gestures for us to come to the booth, obviously more worried about us not paying for our tickets.

As we pass through the entrance, we glimpse a flash of cinnamon-coloured fur go by and we dash up the steps onto the castle wall to try and outwit the dog. Momentarily, we forget about our fluffy stalker and gaze down at the ramshackle houses decorating the dizzyingly steep hillsides sweeping down to the harbour. From up so high, the Aegean and its sky look like a perfect swathe of pale blue silk, except for the long white cotton snags where fishing boats and aeroplanes have left their trails. In the near distance, the tourist island of Thassos looks so lush and green it appears like a tropical rain forest, where jaguars and anteaters and, perhaps, an undiscovered breed of dog roam wild. Then I feel it. Sweaty fur rubs against my legs and I cling onto the wall for support as the dog pushes past. It stops at the next turret along, almost like it's surveying its kingdom and barks several times.

'Bloody hell, if we'd been standing in one of the gaps, he could have easily knocked us over the edge,' says Karly.

I glance down, expecting to see a pile of skeletons in the brambles below us, sun-bleached bony fingers clutching guidebooks and cameras.

'Let's get out of here,' I say.

We hurry back the way we came, aware of the dog trotting along the far wall and down the steps on the opposite side. We scarper towards the tower, and scoot around to the entrance where we come to a sharp stop. A balding man in his 30s is kneeling on the floor, picking up fragments of a broken bottle from what appears to be blood-stained gravel. The stench of cheap red wine hits as we get closer. A shout comes from above us and we glance up at the tower to see a man with a curly ginger mullet waving a small Union Jack flag, whooping in delight.

'Harry! Put them back on. Two women coming up,' says the man, trying to focus on us with bloodshot eyes.

'Sorry, ladeeez. He didn't mean to drop it,' he adds, collapsing onto one knee, proffering the broken glass in the palm of his hands as if he's proposing marriage.

We hear thumping footsteps, followed by a large crash and something heavy sliding down the stairs inside the tower.

'Do you think your friend's all right?' I ask.

'Dunno,' says the man, standing and swaying gently, shards of red and green falling through his fingers back to the ground.

He stumbles over the little bridge leading to the tower steps and vanishes from view. Several moments later, he emerges with his arm around his friend, who is wearing nothing but a pair of Union Jack shorts and an angry red graze along the length of his sunburnt hairy chest. He turns our way and we catch sight of his striking green eyes which almost match lush Thassos below, before the two stagger out of the tower, giggling. We run up the narrow stairs in time to watch the men lurching towards the entrance, our dog running and barking alongside them. The redhead aims a kick at the dog. His trainer scrapes its muzzle and he loses balance, falling flat on his back.

'Serves you right, you drunken pig!' shouts Karly.

The woman rushes out of the ticket booth clutching a large bottle of water. The balding man staggers towards her, assuming she's come to help. But she ignores him and continues to the shaded side of the booth, the dog at her heels. She empties the bottle into a plastic container and stands over the dog protectively, smoothing down its fur as he laps up the water. The redhead, back on his feet, hurries past with his friend, both giving the dog a wide berth. As soon as they disappear into the street, the dog runs after them.

* * *

For lunch we visit our hotel's rooftop bar overlooking the aqueduct and harbour, feeling strangely bereft that the dog didn't come back to the castle for us. We order two large beers and spend the next hour wondering if we'll ever see the dog again. Whether our dog has now been assigned to the drunks, or whether it will suddenly appear on our balcony, or we'll find it under one of our beds, or in the shower. We imagine him taking human form; muscle-bound with tattoo skeletons and semi-naked women riding motorbikes up his forearms, though Karly thinks he's more of a real ale man with a beer belly and a tankard hanging from his belt. Either way, we wonder what he wants from us. Whether word has got out that we're from a dog-loving nation. That we're suckers for furry creatures though Mr Union Jack shorts has obviously put paid to that notion. Maybe that's why he disappeared? He's disappointed by the truth.

* * *

On the way out to the bus station, we silently squeal like we did as teenagers; our dog is slumbering on the welcome mat. I half think about waking him to tell him where we're going. We needn't have worried though because when we stop to salivate over the cakes and pastries in a bakery window, we spot his reflection; he's standing watching us from the pavement opposite. We run to the bus station, a couple of streets away, and jump on board the tourist bus. As we pull away, we wave goodbye to our dog. He's lying in the shade of a magazine kiosk, being petted by a startlingly handsome middle-aged man, smoking a cigar, and when I glance back, I half expect our dog to light up too as he bides his time until we return.

We're visiting the ancient ruins of Philippi, founded by Philip of Macedon, father of Alexander the Great, though he's just as kickass as his son. Philip had managed to quell the tribes surrounding Macedon and establish himself as a military genius by inventing the 18ft long sarissa spear as well as the Macedonian phalanx battle formation, where soldiers line up behind one another in a solid block. Phillip eventually became the most formidable and dominant ruler in the area, almost like the Dogs of Kavala.

The UNESCO site is dogless and practically tourist free, except for a small group of Dutch students and their guide. The ruins are striking, especially the theatre, later rebuilt and expanded during Roman rule. I snap a few photos on my phone, thinking of my poor lost students at home and how they'll politely feign interest when I show them the pictures. I know the Syrians won't be impressed if their reaction to a visit to our local Bronze Age quern stone factory is anything to go by. They'll shrug and say Philippi is nothing compared to the remarkable archaeological sites of Aleppo and Palmyra, now ruins in the truest ever sense of the word, while the Afghans will crack jokes about how the remains resemble their entire country.

'Do you think the Romans made dogs fight?' asks Karly, as we climb the steps, imagining ourselves relegated to the top along with all the other women.

'They pretty much made anything with a heartbeat fight.'

'Oh my God!' says Karly, her mouth dropping open. 'Maybe that's why the dogs in Kavala are so massive. They've been bred from fighting stock over thousands of years. Now they're the boss of everyone with their paws of steel. Have you noticed there are no small dogs?'

'Eaten?'

'And pampered compared to dogs in other areas of Greece. Not a spot of mange, especially compared to the cats.'

It was true. The only cats we'd seen were skinny little things, full of eye infections, always scratching and licking at some unseen parasite. I try and recall some facts from my ancient history degree, so long ago it is almost ancient history too.

'All sorts of nonsense was written about Alexander and his father,' I say. 'Mostly by historians who lived hundreds of years after they died. I remember reading one obscure reference to a tribe who'd been conquered by Philip. They were terrified of him, claiming he turned his most ferocious enemies into hunting dogs.'

'As you do,' says Karly.

'Alexander had a favourite hunting dog called Peritas. It used to go on all his military campaigns, fighting by his side and even saved his life. He was lying on the battlefield injured by a javelin and Peritas was sent out to attack the enemy as a distraction, so they could rescue his master.'

'What about the dog?'

'Killed. Though he got a city in India named after him.'

'Life or a city named after you?' asks Karly.

We'd been playing the same game since primary school.

'Life.'

'Me too.'

'A cat or dog?

'In general, a cat. In Kavala, most definitely a dog,' I say.

* * *

When we leave the hotel for dinner that night, our dog's waiting for us, his fur looking splendidly bouffant like he's had a shampoo and set especially for the weekend. He accompanies us to a bustling seafront restaurant where we sit to watch the sun go down and he settles on the pavement nearby. After dinner, he follows us up the hill towards the castle, home to many lively bars. We choose one playing British punk and new wave music and again sit outside, unworried by the presence of our dog, now reunited with its pack; the Alsatian, the wannabe Shirley Temple, the collie white car hater and a newcomer, much smaller than the others. In fact, it's the first and only small dog we've seen. It's a black Scottie-type whose strange fur arrangement makes us suspect the other dogs have only kept him alive for novelty value, perhaps as a mascot. His coat is as flat and smooth as a pebble on top but half way down it looks as though he's wearing a black tassel skirt.

'What lies beneath?' asks Karly, mysteriously.

The dogs flank the pavements, taking advantage of the cooler air, and as the night wears on, we notice more dogs wander down the hill until there are at least 20 or more lining the pavements, taking turns to doze or patrol the street. The Greeks mostly ignore the dogs, sometimes throwing a lump of meat from their plates to one nearby. But for the most part, the dogs may as well as be part of the street furniture; something to avoid walking into, or tripping over. And for the most part, we ignore them too, happily scoffing the olives and the crisps our waiter keeps bringing us, relishing the fact there are no other tourists around but us.

However, around midnight, we hear familiar shouting echoing around the maze of streets leading from the castle. As it gets closer, the DJ stops the music and an eerie hush descends on our bar, quickly spreading up the street until it seems the whole town is silent. Everyone is staring at the top of the hill where the dogs are lining themselves up into rows four deep, blocking the narrow street like a mini version of Philip's famous battle formation. We watch their furry hackles rise as the shouting gets closer and our dog, right at the front, lets out a strange anguished whimper almost as if he recognises the redhead being hustled out of a side street by a brilliant blue-eyed husky.

'You fucking win, all right?' shouts the man, still wearing his Union Jack shorts, now matched with an England football top.

The man wobbles and steadies himself against a wall, startled to see so many people staring at him in silence.

'What the fuck are you all looking at?' he says, wheeling round and lurching onto the street.

His eyes widen as he spots the husky get in position at the front of the dog phalanx marching towards him.

'John!' he shouts. 'John! Where the fuck are you?'

He staggers backwards, stumbling into the kerb, before running down the hill and disappearing around the corner. The dogs follow, slowly at first until our dog breaks ranks and bounds ahead.

'Do you think he's going to be all right?' Karly asks.

'They'll just give him a scare,' I say, pouring myself another glass of wine. 'Doing us all a favour,' I add though I immediately feel mean for saying so.

The low hum of chatter fills the silence and we watch a striking, amused-looking man stroll up the street to the drumbeat of Devo's *Whip it*. He stops at the table next to us where two elderly portly men are chatting to the waiter. Karly and I glance at one another, recognising him as the same cigar-smoking man who was petting our dog at the bus station. Up close, he's all white teeth and black spidery eyelashes. His friends throw their heads back in laughter as he greets them. The waiter turns to us, smiling, and places a bottle of red wine on our table.

'We didn't order another,' I say.

'On the house,' says the handsome man in perfect English. 'We want our well-behaved guests to enjoy their stay.'

I glance around. Everyone's eyes are on us, their glasses raised in a toast.

'Thank...you,' says Karly.

I force a smile for our audience who seem to be waiting for us to say something.

'To Kavala!' I say, picking up my glass.

'To the dogs of Kavala,' replies the stranger.

Thankfully everyone soon turns back to their conversations. Karly tops up our glasses, though we've barely touched them.

'I don't really want any more,' I whisper, inching my chair closer to hers.

'Me neither. But if we don't drink it, they may set the dogs on us.'

Neither of us laughs and we struggle to make conversation, only too aware the handsome man may be eavesdropping and we may indeed be next. We finish the bottle, though each sip makes me feel more sober and desperate to return to the sanctuary of our hotel room. We bid goodnight to the man and his friends and head down the street arm in arm, feeling dozens of eyes burning into our backs. I'm just about to look back to to see if they're still staring when Karly pulls me against the wall as the pack of dogs gallop by in a blur of fur and teeth. Shirley Temple is at the back, struggling to keep up, and slows long enough for us to see a red hue to the curls around his chops.

'Where's our dog?' asks Karly.

'Perhaps they couldn't resist its tongue any longer,' I say, glancing up and down the street.

'There he is, next to the bins,' says Karly, pointing to the other side of the road where the streetlight has spot lit our dog.

Even though he has his back to us, we can see he's busy eating something and we hold onto each other, thinking the same unspeakable thought; the dogs caught the man and ate him. We creep across the road and Karly digs her nails into my hand as we watch his fat paws needling like a cat at something on the ground. But as we brace ourselves to look closer, we realise he's not eating. With great concentration, he's licking at something, his giant tongue gently, almost lovingly working its way up and down a body of some sort. Whatever it is, it's covered in blood and a thick white substance like the vernix covering new-borns, though as I make out four legs and a long tail, I realise they're far too large to belong to a puppy. The answer arrives after several more tender licks reveal a head of poodle-like ginger fur and two dazzling green eyes staring at us blankly.

The Centring of the Olives

Huxley Harrison thought he would be stuck on olives forever.

For the last six months, he'd stood for seven hours a day placing one slippery black olive onto the centre of each pizza as they sped by on the conveyor belt. This was not how his life was meant to be. Huxley used to have plans. He used to have ambition. Huxley also used to love olives. Plain black or green, stuffed or marinated, especially those filled with chillies. But now he detested them. He couldn't bear to look at their waxy rubber coats. And even the thought of placing one near his mouth filled him with dread.

At first, Huxley hated his fellow workers nearly as much as olives. Not only had they shunned him on the production line, but snubbed any attempts at conversation during lunch and tea breaks. He'd wanted nothing more than to leave King Harry's far behind. But he was trapped by thousands of pounds of debt accrued from a modern history degree and six months of unemployment.

Despite applying for 456 jobs in the media, he'd only had three interviews and no job offers, except for internships on *Paint Removal Monthly* and its sister title, *Cornice Restoration*.

Both roles were unpaid and in London, over two hours away by train. Unlike some of his friends' parents, his were unwilling to help anyone but themselves. His father had left long ago and his mother, although physically in the family home, drank herself absent most days.

So, during his induction day, Huxley could do nothing more than bite his tongue as Audrey, the supervisor, a wiry woman in her 30s with buck teeth, told him how lucky he was to get the job as a factory operative.

'Congratulations Huxley! You beat 203 applicants,' she said. 'It was a close call between you and another young man.'

Audrey leant towards him conspiratorially.

'But he had a few personal hygiene problems,' she said, crinkling her nose in disgust. 'Do you have high hygiene standards, Huxley?'

'Of course,' he said, surreptitiously sniffing his armpits as she turned away to pass him his mug of tea.

He took a sip of the sweet, sickly mixture and his heart sank as he thought about how awful the 201 other applicants must have been. Getting the job had initially cheered Huxley up. He'd been looking forward to earning some money. But Audrey's revelation was like being doused with acid, rapidly dissolving any happiness he'd initially felt.

'He had ideas above his station. Do you have ideas above your station, Huxley?' asked Audrey.

'Modern history wasn't it?' she added, not allowing him to answer. 'Very interesting for a hobby but not very practical in the world of pizzas. We don't need to know why Hitler invaded Poland to make a delicious pepperoni pizza for little Bobby's birthday party. It's all part of our APE.'

'Sorry?' said Huxley suddenly thrown by the introduction of primates into the conversation.

'A-P-E,' she spelled out. 'It's in your induction manual, Huxley. It stands for Ace Pizza Experience. It's what we all strive for, here at King Harry's.'

'Oh,' said Huxley, feeling as though Audrey may as well have smashed his brain in with a sledgehammer.

'Our pizzas lift people's spirits, Huxley. That's all people really want during a recession – a cheap yummy King Harry's Pizza. It helps to take their minds off their money worries and to see the positive things in life.

'This other chap thought pizzas were below him. He had a degree in geography and reckoned he could name every country we source our ingredients from. A bit of a smart Alec, though not so clever at finding his way around the personal hygiene aisles in Boots,' smirked Audrey.

Huxley nodded, noting that the last smidgen of glee had finally left him.

He watched Audrey stare wistfully at the production line while crunching on her ginger nut and hoped this marked the end of Audrey's tirade against further education.

'I told him, you'll never get on with an attitude like that at King Harry's. That's not how I became supervisor,' said Audrey, licking the crumbs from the corners of her mouth with her pointy, lizard-like tongue.

After they'd finished their tea, Audrey showed him around the cavernous factory, full of shiny metal fixtures and fittings and bright white walls covered in signs telling people not to smoke, run or talk.

Huxley had always been curious about the factory. Nearly everyone in the town had a mum, dad, brother, sister, uncle, aunt, cousin or friend who worked at King Harry's. And everyone had a freezer packed full of King Harry pizzas, whether they liked them or not. Huxley had always been struck by the loyalty that King Harry's inspired among its workforce. He'd never heard a bad word uttered about the factory, which sat on the hillside of the pretty seaside town like an ugly scar. However, Huxley always felt there was something malevolent about it, the way the factory consumed most of the town's working population in its 24-hour a day production and the smell of pizza permeating the town, messing with people's appetites. Odder still was how the sea mist's icy fingers chose to clasp onto the factory buildings, leaving nearby streets mist-free and bathed in sunshine, as if it were in league with King Harry to hide the dark arts of pizza making from prying eyes.

Huxley observed the factory operatives expertly paste tomato sauce onto pale doughy bases and sprinkle grated cheese on top.

'It's an art form isn't it, Huxley?' said Audrey as they both stared in admiration at the mysterious gloved hands tossing pizza bases through a small square window from the bakery onto the production line.

'You can work your way up to the bakery but first things first, you'll start on the olive station,' said Audrey, taking him to the end of the production line where a squat, middle-aged man was placing an olive in the centre of each pizza as they sped past.

The man dipped a pudgy hand into the vat of black olives in front of him and deftly grabbed a handful. His fat fingers were surprisingly agile as they delicately placed an olive in the centre of each pizza. After five minutes, Huxley was allowed to take over the task but found himself unable to keep up with the speed of the conveyor belt and several pizzas whizzed by olive-less. The production line stopped. Everyone turned to look at Huxley. He felt himself blushing. Audrey came rushing over.

'It's okay, Huxley. We'll keep it slower this morning. By this afternoon, you'll have the hang of it,' said Audrey.

Huxley didn't know where to look. He felt useless and pathetic. He couldn't even put an olive on a pizza properly. No wonder no-one had wanted to employ him, he thought to himself.

However, within ten minutes, Huxley had got the hang of centring olives and Audrey gave the nod for the production line to speed up. Huxley assumed he'd be moved onto another task like the other operatives who swapped stations every hour. But on the second day, Huxley was again put on the olive station and enviously watched the other operatives switch from cheese sprinkling to tomato pasting from pepperoni placing to pine-apple chunk arranging. At night, he even began to dream he was sleeping on a luxurious bed made of tomato sauce with a blanket made of grated cheese that he'd have to sprinkle over himself, without gloves.

At the end of his third day, he'd put his extended olive duty down to an impromptu visit by Fatcat Supermarkets, who were doing a spot check on the production of their new range aimed at young girls, Princess Pizzas. Huxley assumed that Audrey had wanted to keep the new boy on a simple task so that he wouldn't mess up the production line during their visit. Princess Pizzas were regular-sized pizzas covered in tomato sauce, with a pink olive in the middle, finished off with a sprinkling of edible gold and silver glitter. After being wrapped in plastic, they were then inserted into pink boxes decorated with pictures of a benevolent King Harry and his beautiful flaxen-haired daughter, Princess Margareta. Huxley understood. He didn't want to ruin Audrey's perfect production line either. So, he stood all day placing his olives slap bang in the centre of each pizza that flew past.

On day four, he put his enforced olive centring down to an oversight by Audrey after all the excitement of the Princess Pizzas. But by day five, it suddenly dawned on Huxley that he was still in training. Audrey had quite clearly left him there because he was not up to doing any other pizza-making related tasks.

At morning tea break, he plucked up the courage to ask a kindly-looking lady in her 60s, who had once smiled at him in the canteen, how long it would be before he was taken off olives. But as soon as he approached her, she scuttled into the toilets. Initially stunned by her reaction, he felt a rage burn through him and hid around the corner of the toilets to ambush her.

'Why am I always on olives?' he demanded when she emerged.

'You're the new olive boy,' she whispered, glancing around nervously.

'What do you mean, the new olive boy?'

All sorts of hideous images flashed though his mind. Did this mean he would be the olive boy forever? That this was all he would ever achieve? And most importantly, what had happened to the old olive boy? Had King Harry executed him for not centring the olives?

'Shhh! Keep your voice down. They watch and hear everything. We're never alone at King Harry's.'

Huxley followed her vacant blue eyes around the room where they flickered up to the ceiling. Four cameras were focused on them. Huxley stormed over to Audrey's office and knocked at the door.

'What can I do for you, Huxley?' asked Audrey, not bothering to look up at her visitor.

'I'd like to do something other than olives please.'

'Do you want this job, Huxley? Because as I said there are hundreds out of there who'd bite your hand off for a job here,' she said, finally looking up.

'Well, yes,' swallowed Huxley, remembering all the unopened bills littering the kitchen table at home.

'Well, let's not run before we've learnt to walk.'

'But it's just putting olives on a pizza.'

'Oh, is it now!' said Audrey, standing up from her chair sharply and marching towards Huxley. "That's exactly what he said.'

'Who said?'

'Your predecessor. The old olive boy.'

'What happened to him?'

'He couldn't centre.'

'What do you mean?'

'He kept missing.'

'How can you not centre?'

'Exactly! I like your attitude, Huxley,' Audrey said as she glanced at her watch. 'Tea break over. Back to work now. You go and show us how you can centre those olives, boy!'

* * *

After two weeks of being on the olive station, Huxley began to understood why the old olive boy hadn't been able to centre. His fingers were refusing to do what he told them. They were aching from being in the same position day in day out. At night, he even bathed them in a bowl of hot water to ease the muscle cramps. They wanted to be stretched. They were threatening to go on strike. And on day 29, Huxley gave into their demands. He looked around furtively and then placed two olives just off centre, then another three and four, until the pizzas were decorated with five olives spread in a cross. Someone, somewhere would get a big olive surprise, Huxley smiled to himself. He felt his heart bursting with joy at the thought that his olive formation was probably ground-breaking, that it had probably never been attempted at King Harry's before. He didn't care if he got into trouble. He felt free for the first time in weeks.

A few moments later, a collective groan arose from the factory workers as the production line ground to a halt. Everyone looked across at Huxley accusingly. Some were even nodding their heads in disgust.

'I don't need to tell an intelligent young man like you, Huxley, that the olive is an integral part of the APE,' said Audrey, who had escorted him into her office for his own safety.

'We don't like people messing with our magic formula. And they,' she said, gesturing to the workers glaring at the office, "don't like being messed around.'

'The olive is why Fatcat Supermarkets buy our pizzas for 50 pence each and are able to sell them to their customers for £4.99. An olive screams quality, Huxley. It brings a bit of class into the little people's lives. It's like finding a Belgian praline in a cheap box of fruit centres. People do not want to see five olives on their pizzas. With one olive, they think they're lucky. If we give them five, they will think: why not six or seven? Comprende?'

'Yes,' muttered Huxley, his heart sinking further than he ever thought possible.

'All you need to remember is that the olive is King Harry's signature. And King Harry is like a god round here. You don't want to anger a god, do you, Huxley?' said Audrey, who was standing so close he could smell the custard cream she'd just eaten.

'No,' said Huxley, feeling his bottom lip wobble.

'Well then, centre the olives, Huxley, and King Harry may find it in his heart to forgive you. But first of all what do you say to King Harry?'

'Sorry,' mumbled Huxley.

'Say it like you mean it,' shouted Audrey. 'Prostrate yourself before our King.'

Huxley fell to his knees. 'I'm sorry, King Harry.'

'Go APE, Huxley! I know you've got it in you,' said Audrey, patting him on his back.

Huxley resisted the urge to shove Audrey away and tell her where he'd like to stick her precious pizzas. He had a brain. He had ambition. He wanted a proper job where he could shine.

But he remembered the final reminder for the gas bill that his mother still hadn't paid.

'But...but when can I do something else, like cheese sprinkling?'

'Your time will come. King Harry will know when you're ready.'

* * *

Six months later, when Huxley arrived for work, Audrey and all the operatives were gathered in the locker room. As he opened the door, they erupted into cheers and applause. Some were even punching the air with joy.

'Congratulations Huxley!' said Audrey, thrusting a pizza-shaped piece of paper at him. 'You've done us proud. We're moving you onto cheese.'

Huxley felt himself turn puce at the attention. He looked down at the piece of paper in his shaky hands. It was a certificate. It read: *You've gone APE on the Olive Station. Well done!* It had even been signed by King Harry himself with his beautiful, sloping, majestic signature.

'If you make a good job of cheese, the world is your oyster, Huxley. Come here.'

Audrey grabbed Huxley and squeezed him tightly.

'I knew you had it in you,' she whispered.

Huxley forced himself to smile as he looked up at the cameras. King Harry may be watching. Anyway, why shouldn't he be pleased with himself? Why shouldn't he enjoy the warm feeling of accomplishment spreading through his body, and before he knew it, he found himself grinning at the cameras.

But then a troubling thought reared its ugly head. Would he be up to the job? His fingers had eventually knuckled down to some hard work after their rebellion but would they be able rise to the challenge and be flexible enough to sprinkle cheese? Doubts crashed in on Huxley and he felt faint. All the operatives filed past him, each and every one of them had snubbed him as the new olive boy, but now stopped to shake his hand and offer words of congratulations and encouragement.

'You sit for a few minutes, Huxley. It's a lot to take in. Then I'll get you acquainted with the grated cheese,' said Audrey.

'But who's going to do the olives?' asked Huxley, panicking.

'Don't worry,' said Audrey, patting his head. 'We have a new olive girl.'

A few minutes later, Huxley shook with joy as he donned his plastic gloves and plunged his hands into a gigantic tub of the grated cheese, feeling its coldness running between his fingers. He closed his eyes in ecstasy.

'Feels good, doesn't it?' Audrey whispered.

Huxley nodded and glanced over at the olive station. The new olive girl was hard at work. She was young, maybe just 18. Her white overalls hung off her bony frame, her harsh profile partially hidden by the King Harry's regulation cap. Huxley felt a sudden stab of pity as he watched her concentrating on centring each olive, and wondered if the thought of being stuck on olives forever had crossed her mind yet.

But he couldn't spare the time to worry about the new girl. He had bigger fish to fry. Huxley had to focus on scooping out the exact amount of cheese required by King Harry for each pizza.

That afternoon, just as he was feeling confident in his sprinkling abilities, the production line stopped. Everyone, including Huxley, immediately knew where the fault lay. They stared across at the new olive girl who was hunched over the conveyor belt, sobbing. She had somehow managed to knock over the vat of olives which were scuttling over the belt and floor like baby cockroaches.

Huxley tutted. At this rate he would never get onto the tomato sauce station.

Camping with Daddy

You kept glancing in as you walked past. And I pretended to be fascinated with the pub wall, how the bits between the bricks were filled with insect legs and wings caught in spider webs.

I wanted to wake Dad and tell him the pub's being held up by spiders and we should move in case it tumbles down on top of our car. But if I did, I'd have to turn and look at you and your friend.

Nosy parker alert! I blurt out, hoping Dad would sit up. Take notice. Because there's nothing he hates more. He'd give you and your friend a mouthful. Tell you to mind your own business. And you'd scuttle away across the cobbles, hobble, hobble, in your fancy stilettos. And we'd laugh at you when your spiky heels got trapped between the stones and you fell flat on your faces.

The thought of you and your friend flailing around the cobbles among the dog shit and chippy papers makes me brave and I turn to look at you. But you've gone. I spy you further up the road, tottering towards the next pub, *The Lifeboat*. I peer at the sign. It's of a man in a tiny rubber dingy being swept away by a gigantic wave, and I think, what kind of rubbish rescue service is that? It's more like one of the boats the illegals litter the beach with. You've stopped under the sign now. Heads together. Chatter, chatter. And I wonder if you're talking about the rubbish lifeboat, or me and Dad.

Tittle tattle. Gossips. Trouble makers. You women, always sticking your noses in where they're not wanted, says Dad. You ain't going to be like that are you, Lills?

And then I see you put your hand over your mouth and glance back as if you've forgotten something really important. I remember Dad doing the same when he opened his stash box one morning and saw Josh's jam sandwich staring back at him. I'd never seen him move so fast. Sprinted all the way up Dover Road to the nursery. Ten minutes later he was back, collapsed on the sofa, nursing his stash box in his lap, laughing his head off even when Jan kicked us out. I laughed a little bit too. But out of relief because Josh was like my little brother for a while.

The sun is streaming through the windows. I wipe away the sweat from my upper lip, trying not to breathe in the stench of Dad's lager breath and body odour. I want to open a window. But Dad told me not to and I'm frightened I may die like a dog or one of those babies you hear about being left in cars on a hot sunny day. I lean across and millimetre by millimetre ease the window down until I'm gulping in the air like it's water and notice a sea mist has fallen like a curtain, blocking out France.

The next thing I see is you and your friend clickety-clacking towards us until you're level with my window, waving. I shift across to the other side and watch the swirling mist hiding the harbour arm and the top of the fishing boats, trapped by the low tide. I feel your eyes on me and wish it would hurry along and make us invisible too.

I hear your friend telling you to leave it. Walk away, she says. Don't get involved.

Yes, walk away, I think, and keep walking.

I stare at the lines on the back of Dad's sunburnt neck. They're so thick they look like scars where someone once tried to slice his head off.

Are you okay? you say and I reach across and wind up the window quickly so Dad doesn't hear.

I'm doing you a favour here, lady. You don't want to wake a sleeping dragon.

You knock on the window.

Your friend hangs back, saying, come on, we're going to be late.

Yeah, but she should be at school, I hear you say, and I smile to myself because I haven't been to school for weeks now. Not since Dad took me camping. A trip to the seaside, how do you like that, Lills? Just me and you. We'll camp out at the coastal park and take a few of those disposable barbecues. It'll be an adventure. But I knew the real reason. I'd read the eviction letters and Dad forgets I had to tell the bailiffs he was out while he hid behind the sofa.

Just you and me, he kept saying until his long lost mate turned up on the second night. My best friend, an old mate from before, he'd said. Before what? I'd wanted to ask. But I don't ask. Questions are for nosy parkers like you, lady, with your killer heels. I've leant not to ask questions.

So when this man turns up and Dad has to ask him his name even though he's his best mate, I wonder what kind of camping holiday he has in mind. Because it would be all right if it were just me and Dad. But this man has to ruin it, going off into the bushes with Dad and his precious Tupperware box, coming back all happy and harmless.

Then on the third night, he doesn't go with Dad. He stays with me by the fire. Protect you from the wolves, he jokes, ruffling my hair. But I wonder who's going to protect me from him. Because when Dad crashes back through the undergrowth, all spaced out and passes out in the tent, the ruffles turn into strokes, the jokes into comments like; if you put on a bit of make-up you'd be a real looker and I can't believe you're only 12 'cause you look a lot older.

He says he has a nice warm caravan and why don't I sleep there with him and I won't have to wake up with the slugs in my sleeping bag. I'd rather sleep in a slug nest than sleep anywhere near you Mr Big Fat Slug. I shout it. I do. But Dad can't hear me. He's out cold. And the slug man knows it.

And there you are again. Banging on the window now. I distract myself with Dad's fat neck lines wondering if they have any significance like the lines on our palms. When Mum was around old Mrs Bishop, our neighbour, used to read ours. The right hand is the one you're born with. The left tells you what you'll make of yourself, she'd say, grabbing at mine with her knobbly fingers. She taught me how to turn your left hand into a fist and count the wrinkles by your little finger to find out how many babies you'll have. I recheck mine and see all my future children are thick with grime. She said I'd live in a nice house. Said I'm going to do all right for myself and I laugh at that thinking if only you could see me now Mrs Bishop.

I turn to see you mouthing, Are you okay?

And tears come, from I don't know where, and I'm trying to kill them, because Dad may wake up and see me crying.

Open the window, you say, you're going to boil to death.

And you're right. My head feels like it's going to explode. My mouth's so dry I'm tempted to open one of Dad's stinky lagers.

I lean over all the half-eaten pizzas in their boxes, yellow cheese turning green with mould, the pile of dirty clothes and unopened pound shop barbecues, and wind down the window half way. I close my eyes, enjoying the sea mist's icy fingers wiping my face cool. I hear a tin can tap dance down the pavement somewhere nearby, accompanied by my growling stomach as the smell of fish and chips waft in.

When I open my eyes I see you've stepped back onto the pavement. You look like you're sucking lemons. And I'm pleased I'm so hot and red-faced otherwise you'd see me blushing.

Jesus, your friend says, the state.

What's your name, you ask again and again. How old are?

And I look at you properly for the first time. I reckon you're like Mrs Bishop's future version of me, sorted with three cute kids, nice house, new clothes, loving husband, foreign holidays.

Is that your Father? you ask.

And for a moment the word confuses me.

No, he isn't, I say. He's my Dad, and then as the words leave me, I realise it's the same thing and I nod.

Is he okay? Is your Dad okay?

I glance round to see your friend hovering in the background again. She's talking into her mobile, holding it to her ear with perfectly manicured red shiny nails she doesn't want to dirty with me and Dad.

I think he needs help, you say.

And I feel pinpricks of fear running through me now because I thought he was just sleeping. But now I don't know. Maybe he isn't. He's been out for ages. We came early morning for breakfast, but it was midsummer sunrise early and nothing was open. Dad disappeared into the public toilets next to the fish shop and came out staggering all over the place. He collapsed in the driving seat, slurring orders to close the windows, lock the doors, not to talk to anyone.

I tap Dad's arm, ready for him to turn suddenly and say, ha, ha got you good, Lills. Scared you, didn't I?

But he stays dead still, head lolling on his chest. I lurch forward to shake his shoulder and my hand stops mid air because two amber eyes are staring at me. His tiger tattoo has its mouth wide open, ready to bite.

Dad! Wake up! I shout.

He's going to get into trouble for this. I know it and I push his tiger-free shoulder so hard that he falls slowly onto the passenger seat, his head resting on the 12 pack of lager as if it's the world's comfiest pillow.

Dad! Wake up! I scream and feel the hot liquid running down my legs.

It's soothing at first like a hot bath. But in a moment I know it'll feel sticky and start to smell.

I glance up at you then. Your eyes are wide with panic. It must be catching because I feel it too and my mind is blank. I can't remember my name until I glimpse the sloping black ink on Dad's wrist.

Lilly, I say. My name's Lilly.

Lilly? My sister's called Lilly, you say. And I watch your mouth as it tries to smile but keeps collapsing like one of my rubbish sandcastles. Rising, falling, rising, falling until you say, it's going to be okay, Lilly. Open the door.

Long listed for the Colm Tóibín International Short Story Award 2016.

Hideous Claws of Gruesome Monsters

Hideous claws of gruesome monsters line the roads in these parts. They're dried up cacti really, but I prefer to think of them as beasts trying to escape Spain's baking interior, migrating to the cooler Atlantic coast every summer along with all the city folk.

They're meant to be the Iron Man of plants but even they can't survive this heatwave. The only vegetation alive are the pale pink, bulbous flowers blooming on the verges like regular show offs. I make a mental note to investigate the flowers. But not now. It's 42 degrees Celsius and nothing could get me out of this air conditioned car. Besides, Natalie is in full swing. It'd be rude to interrupt. To stop the car, jump out and let all the hot air in, though she generates plenty of her own.

'I said, 'You're turning into your father. He who died of alcohol poisoning, remember? The man who abandoned your mother for drink,' and you know what he said?'

I don't bother answering. I know what's coming.

'But you're abandoning me!' Jesus. He just does not get it.'

I make sympathetic noises while resisting the urge to turn the wheel and drive into the oncoming car.

'Talk about making it all my fault.'

'Alcoholics always blame everyone else for their problems,' I say, feebly for what seems the millionth time.

'Exactly. I drive him to drink, apparently.'

She glances over at me, letting out a laugh similar to a horse's welcome snicker.

'What a charmer,' I say.

'He ruined every party by getting drunk. One time he even stole someone's bike and tried to ride home. Six in the morning I get a call from the hospital. Your husband has had an accident, Mrs Frobisher, broken both legs. Idiot cycled off a railway bridge. He can't even remember getting up there.'

'Surprised he didn't kill himself.'

'Perish the thought,' Natalie says, nudging me on the arm. 'And it was always me who had to apologise for his behaviour. If I tried to get an apology out of him he'd stop talking to me...'

'Very nice of him.'

'Tell me about it. I just had to look at him sometimes and he'd start. Raging about a sock I hadn't picked up, or not putting the bins out, or the dishwasher not loaded correctly. 'What have you been doing all day?' he'd yell.'

'Bastard.'

Natalie takes in a deep breath and sighs.

'You never did meet him, did you? Didn't come to our wedding.'

'I was away working, wasn't I?' I say, bracing myself for another telling off.

'I thought you'd make the effort. Sally Richards didn't find it too hard.'

'She was in Italy. I was in Brazil,' I say, slowing and turning onto the dust road leading to El Palmar beach.

'Mmm. I suppose,' she says, pausing for a moment. 'I wasn't sure you'd reply to my friend request, let alone come on holiday.'

'Why not?'

'It's been 21 years. I could have asked any of my friends but when I saw your Facebook update, I thought, Ah, bless. That woman needs a holiday. Anyway, we used to have a laugh, didn't we? Remember Mr Giddings? Go on, you do it,' she says, nudging my elbow again. 'You always did the best impressions.'

I bring my elbow in and force a smile. 'One-two-three-STOP!' I say in a bad South African accent.

Natalie snorts laughter through her nose and bangs the top of the glove box so hard it pops open which sets her off even more.

'I said you'd be a laugh to go with,' she says, wiping her eyes before slamming the glove box closed. 'One-two-three-stop, Jamie. You've gone past our parking space.'

'I think we should use a car park today,' I say. 'That man got a bit angry.'

'Talk about over the top. He said it was his shop. But was it really? It was closed when we got there. Maybe we'd just stolen his regular beach parking space.'

'I think it was his shop. He had keys to get in. It was the end of siesta,' I say, turning into a field next to one of the many beach bars lining the road. 'And to be fair, we didn't leave much space for customers to get in or out of the door.'

'You can pay for it then,' says Natalie, folding her arms over her handbag, nodding over at the pony-tailed young man, emerging from a little wooden hut.

I wind down the window, take three euros out of my change purse and hand it over.

'I hope he's the official parking attendant. Make sure you get a receipt,' says Natalie.

The man passes over a piece of paper. 'Until four in the morning,' he says, grinning.

'But we're only here for a couple of hours,' Natalie shouts in my ear. 'See if you can get it cheaper.'

'Gracias,' I say, quickly pulling away to find a space.

* * *

The next day, we return to the same parking spot. But as we head down the wooden walkway, through the dunes and onto the beach, we come under fire. Fierce gusts of wind blast us with wave after wave of sand.

'It's blinding me!' says Natalie, throwing her towel over her head.

'This must be the Levante,' I say, shielding my face with my beach bag. 'I think we've been lucky. It can blow for days and even weeks.'

'The travel agent didn't mention that,' says Natalie.

I glance up and down miles of white sandy beach, watching the dry sand dancing in the wind, creating patterns of stretch marks and scratches.

'Well, we're here now. We can go for a quick swim at the very least,' I say, comforted to see a few holidaymakers have determinedly set up camp with wind breaks and umbrellas dug deep into the sand.

We scuttle to a static wooden beach umbrella and dump our bags underneath, Natalie squealing as the wind hurls handfuls of sand at our bare legs. I can't wait to lie down and sleep, sand-storm or no sandstorm, after being kept awake three nights in a row by Natalie's snoring. I'm just wondering how many more sleepless nights I can cope with, or whether to start taking the pills again when a tall young African man, dressed in a long white robe and carrying a bundle of colourful beach throws, appears. He drops the bundle and snatches my throw from the top of my beach bag, tying its ends into the gaps in the umbrella.

'Excuse me! That's not going to do much good,' says Natalie. 'It's going to flap around.'

He ignores Natalie and secures one end around the shade, then bends down and begins shovelling sand over the flapping ends until we have a wind break. With a flash of gappy white teeth, he gestures to the shelter as if inviting us into his home.

'Gracias. Cuánto cuesta?' I ask, gesturing at his throws.

'Quinze,' he says, taking out several to show us.

'Jamie, don't encourage him. He'll see how much money you've got and steal it.'

'Natalie. Stop.'

'God, he must have seen you coming.'

My eyes are drawn to a white throw decorated with an intri-cate blue tree, its branches weaving in and out of each other. It reminds me of a picture Michael once bought me of the spiritual tree of life. I hand him the cash and after he puts the money away in his bum bag, he lays the throw down for us in our new shelter, his face etched in such concentration it's as if he's performing brain surgery. And I wonder at the randomness of birth. If he'd been born in the UK, then perhaps he would be a brain surgeon. But here he was selling beach throws to ungrateful tourists. The photos I'd seen in the newspaper *Diario de Cadiz* at breakfast flash into my head; five bodies had been washed ashore, along with a tiny rubber dingy, just outside Cadiz and I wonder if this man had made a similar treacherous journey across the Straits of Gibraltar.

'Cuál país?'

'Jamie!'

'Sudan. South,' he says. 'And you are Germany?'

'Excuse me! We are not German,' says Natalie, hands on hips. 'English.'

'Most Germans and Spanish here,' he says, as a way of an apology, picking up his wears. 'Enjoy your holiday.'

I lie down on the tree of life while Natalie stands, watching him walk further down the beach, stopping to show his throws to an extended Spanish family.

'They shouldn't be allowed on the beach.'

'You can't stop people coming onto a public beach.'

'It doesn't make it very relaxing.'

'I can't imagine it's very relaxing in South Sudan at the moment.'

'Not my problem. I'm going for a swim. Make sure you keep an eye on my stuff.'

I turn on my tummy feeling it knot, berating myself for forgetting why I never kept in touch with Natalie. Memories cascade over me like the grains of sand. I watch her, still wrapped up in her towel, tentatively dip her feet into the sea, remembering how she'd cornered the market in failed relationships from an early age as well as one-night stands, STDs, rubbish landlords, thieving boyfriends and betrayals. No-one else was allowed to have a drama around Natalie. Hers belonged to the Premier League. Everyone else's the Third Division. She'd seemed exciting and reckless when we were teenagers but now just sad. Her bad choices had aged her prematurely despite the bleached blonde bob, fake tan and botox. At school, I'd been envious of her beautiful almost translucent skin which was now mottled with worm-like thread veins. And every time she spoke, I imagined those worms desperately trying to find her lost youth and something else too; her kindness. Because she had been kind once, hadn't she? Then I shock myself thinking perhaps, it is me who is changed. Had I once been like her?

* * *

'I have affinity with orkas,' says Natalie. 'Free Willy is my favourite film.'

'That's very nice,' says our guide, a young petite woman with excellent English. 'We can guarantee you will see pilot wales and dolphins but we can't guarantee orkas,' she explains to us and the other customers, two families with several angelic-faced children.

'It is likely?' asks Natalie.

'A reasonable chance,' says the guide. 'And you won't get another opportunity this week. We're lucky today as the Levante has calmed but it's forecast to get stronger tonight for a few days and will be too dangerous for the boats to go out.'

'Oh, come on, Natalie. We're here now.'

'It's a lot of money for a 'reasonable chance'. You promised we'd see orkas, Jamie.'

'I don't think I ever promised we'd see them, Natalie. I was just reading from the guidebook. It said they pass through the Straits of Gibraltar in July and August.'

Despite wearing her diamante-studied designer sunglasses, I can feel her eyes burning into me and the familiar band around my head tightening. A migraine is threatening, pummelling hand into fist.

'Why don't I pay? A thank you for the holiday.'

I hand over 100 euros for the three-hour tour from Tarifa and we receive two photocopied leaflets. One side showcases what species we need to look for, while there's a whale and dolphin word search and crossword on the other side.

Natalie hustles me outside.

'Let's wait here. We can push to the front and get plum seats away from the kids,' she says, nodding her head towards the two families inside.

'I think it's quite a small boat,' I say. 'I don't think you can avoid them.'

'I know but if we take up enough space they won't be able to sit with us. Children are little vomit machines. There were two on our snorkelling trip in Mexico a few years back and they were sick over the side of the boat. All the pretty little fishes we were watching gobbled it all up,' says Natalie, grimacing. 'I've never been able to look at tropical fish in the same way.'

A few minutes later, the tour guide emerges from the office followed by the rest of the group. Natalie grabs my elbow, her long, red acrylic nails scratch my skin as she drags me to the front of the queue. When we get to the boat, she pulls me to the back and places her handbag on the seat next to her.

We set sail and I lose myself in the inky blueness of the Atlantic, enjoying the cooler air, thinking of how Michael would have loved it here. How he would have taken the piss out of Natalie and warned me about accepting a free holiday from someone I hadn't seen for years. I understand you're desperate to get away from everything, I hear him whispering. But did you have to go with her? Anyway, you can never get away from yourself, Jamie. Me not being here is something you have to learn to live with. But the problem is Michael is everywhere, even in Spain, whether it's in the gait of another man, or a smile from a random stranger. I close my eyes, hoping Natalie will remain quiet. But before long, I feel a familiar nudging at my elbow. I swallow the urge to elbow her back twice as hard.

'Trouble ahead.'

I open my eyes to see two of the cute blonde boys, wobbling along the gangway towards us. There's only room for one person to sit at the back; two if Natalie moves her bag. The older one sits down on the spare seat, beckoning for his little brother to sit on his lap.

'Sweet,' I smile and lean across Natalie to pick up her bag. 'Sit here.'

Natalie nudges me again, her elbow sharp in my ribs. 'What you do that for?'

She stands. 'Swap seats then, Mother Theresa.'

I gladly swap and turn my back on Natalie as the guide comes over and points out a school of dolphins, all plentiful pink, grey and yellow flashes as they dive in and out of black-blue waves.

Then a flying fish scoots over the dolphins' heads, shimmering like a disco ball, as if to say, Look at me, suckers, I can fly further than any of you losers.

The two boys glance at me, huge grins stretched across their faces.

'Wow! I never realised they could fly so far!' says the older boy.

'It looked so pleased with itself,' says his brother.

'I didn't see it,' I hear Natalie in my ear. 'Anyway, fish can't be pleased with themselves, for goodness sake.'

The little boy frowns.

'Of course they can,' I say.

The boys look away as the guide excitedly points across to our right. 'Pilot whales!'

The boat turns slightly in order to catch them up before the captain cuts the engine and we bob gently up and down. A few moments later, the sea around us starts bubbling up as black fins slice up through the water. We lean over the side, watching one of the whales disappearing underneath the boat.

'Sinister-looking creatures,' says Natalie. 'Like they're wearing gimp suits.'

'I think they're beautiful,' I say, mesmerised by their shiny black skin.

And then they vanish, scared off by the ferry to Tangier passing nearby. I feel slightly sick as our boat is tossed around by the ferry's wake and I think again of the newspaper photos of the migrants washed up on the beach and how terrifying it must be to cross this stretch of water in an overcrowded boat. After a few minutes, the sea calms enough for us to pick up speed back to Tarifa.

'But we haven't seen any orkas!' says Natalie as the guide walks by.

'The pilot whales and dolphins have been ganging up on the orkas recently, driving them out of their territory, so we haven't seen them so often this year,' she explains.

'But the orkas are loads bigger,' says the little boy next to me.

'Ah, but pilot whales are more aggressive,' says the guide.

'You should have told us that before we paid. I think you should give our money back.'

'Natalie. Leave it,' I say wondering if pilot whales enjoy human flesh.

'But they advertise it as an orka watch!'

'The brochure says we never guarantee you'll see any sea creatures,' says the guide, walking away.

'Always get you on the small print,' says Natalie, who turns around and kneels on the seat, gazing out to sea.

If I was to reach out and push, she would easily fall over the edge and disappear into the churned up, white foam and perhaps, into the belly of an undiscerning pilot whale.

* * *

The sunset is over quickly thanks to the Levante returning with a vengeance and mustering all the clouds. But it has kindly left a letterbox-shaped shaft of orange light in the sky. I imagine posting a letter through it, asking all the gods of the world if they know where Michael is because I don't. I'm up there in the clouds trying to peer through the letterbox when a voice breaks in.

'That was so amazing.'

Natalie slumps down next to me on the sofa, before sitting up and grabbing a handful of olives.

'Massage good?' I ask, closing my eyes and trying to stay in the clouds.

'Heavenly,' she says. 'Though these images of Bob kept flashing up.'

'Images?'

'You know, just as you drift off. He had his crazed bunny face on.'

'What?'

'It's a face he pulls when he gets cross. We used to laugh about it but now it's just disturbing. He looked really angry. Like he wanted to kill me. It must have been the text messages he sent this morning. I suppose we'll have to give him the money back.'

My eyes snap open.

'What money?'

'The money for the holiday. Your half.'

'But I thought he didn't want to come?'

'No, I didn't want him to come. And I suppose he did pay for it.'

I sit up straight.

'Natalie.'

'It's all right. I've given him your email address. He said he'd take monthly instalments. It's not as if you haven't had a nice time, is it?' she says, popping my last olive into her mouth. 'What do you want to do for dinner tonight?'

'I think I have a migraine coming,' I say, closing my eyes again.

'Well, make sure it's gone by tomorrow. It's our last day and I want a decent night on the tiles.'

* * *

The next morning, I wake to find Natalie gone. It's 9.50am and breakfast is about to finish. I dress as quickly as I can, trying to shake off the sleeping pill haze. When I emerge from the lift into reception, I hear Natalie before I see her.

'Worst massage I've ever had,' she says.

'I'm sorry to hear that, madam,' says the young man at reception. 'Our therapists are very experienced and we've never had any complaints before.'

'Maybe because your standards are lower than ours. I want a full refund.'

'I can give you 50 per cent off another treatment.'

'And I can give you a terrible review on Trip Advisor,' says Natalie.

I tip-toe past into the dining room and find a small table at the edge of the terrace next to the garden, behind a large family sitting around several large tables. I order coffee and sink down in my seat, out of view. That's when I spot the miracle pink bulbous flowers I'd seen on the side of the road next to the monster claws. They're decorating an overgrown patch of land next to the pool's changing area. I check Natalie isn't nearby and get up to investigate. Except when I go to touch the flowers, my fingers recoil because they're not flowers but snails. Hundreds of them sucking the moisture out of these shrivelled brown weeds. Tears pool as I slump back in my chair, wondering why I thought Natalie, like the snails, was something she could never be. There's a good reason why you never kept in touch, whispers Michael. I know, I never even liked her, I think to myself. I was the new girl. She was my crimped-haired crusader defending me from the bullies. But it wasn't out of altruism, I soon realised. She didn't have any other friends. I was someone to hang out with and boss around.

I wonder whether I can get a flight home. Then I realise I only have one more day. I can bear one more day surely, until I spot Natalie at the buffet, tossing bread rolls and chocolate croissants into a large plastic bag.

* * *

Natalie tracks me down as I walk to the beach through the hotel grounds.

'Result! Full refund and new acrylics,' she says, thrusting her shiny red claws under my eyes.

'But you said you enjoyed the massage yesterday.'

'At the time. But afterwards, I realised there were crucial areas of the massage that were underwhelming. The therapist won't learn unless she knows where she's going wrong.'

'So you're doing her a favour,' I say, trying to block out her voice by tuning into the rustling of the pine forest nearby and the roar of the sea as the Levante strengthens.

'Yes, I like to think so,' says Natalie as we climb down the steps onto the sand.

For a moment, we watch the wind whipping the sea into froth at the shore, while further out it's slapping waves into each other, creating headless beasts reaching out of the sea with their foamy fingers.

'I'm not sure about this beach today. Look at all that seaweed.'

'It's the sea.'

'I don't like the feel of it. Like greasy little hands groping you under water.'

'You should be so lucky.'

'Funny!' says Natalie, elbowing me hard. 'I have my fair share of admirers. In fact, I've got a very special one. He almost came with me.'

I hurry along, feeling sick at the thought I was probably a last minute choice as a holiday companion to Natalie's seedy affair.

'Don't you want to know all the juicy details?' she calls out.

'No,' I say as two paramedics sprint past and jump over the wooden fence separating the hotel from the beach.

'I was looking forward to telling you all about it. He's a lovely man. But it's a bit awkward -.'

'I wonder what's happened?' I interrupt as we round the corner, and see two police cars parked next to a large rock exposed by the low tide.

Several policemen are chatting to two lifeguards, all staring at something hidden by the rock.

'Probably some old Spanish geezer dragged under by the weight of his body hair. Anyway, as I was saying, it's difficult because I know his wife. She's in my Zumba class.'

I spin round to face her.

'You know what, Natalie, you haven't asked me one single question about Michael or how I'm coping,' I say, batting away my tears with the new throw before turning my back to her.

'We're on holiday. I...I didn't want to upset you,' I hear Natalie say behind me.

I follow the two paramedics who disappear behind the rock just as a policeman appears from the other side. He's walks over to the hotel's wooden fence and with difficulty ties a piece of yellow tape to it before retracing his steps and securing the other end under a rock.

'For God sake! Why did they have to cordon off the bit without seaweed?' says Natalie.

I crane my neck trying to peek around the rock until I see two bodies lying on the sand on their backs as if dozing in the sun.

'That's how I found Michael. His arms flung out across the bed. I thought he was taking an afternoon nap at first. He looked so peaceful, and that's what hurts so much; he looked like he was pleased he'd gone,' I say, as Natalie catches up with me.

'Bloody illegals. Why did they have to get washed up on our beach, on our last day?' she says.

She takes out her mobile from her bag, pouts and snaps a selfie with the men's bodies and police visible in the background.

I feel Michael then. The warmth of his strong arms wrapped around my waist, holding me. Go on. I dare you, he whispers.

I don't need his encouragement though because I've already snatched her phone and throw it hard, surprised by the perfect arc it makes as it flies through the air, before disappearing into the horror of monsters, their watery claws reaching up to claim it.

Long listed for the Commonwealth Short Story Prize 2019.

The Potato Eaters

I wake to the smell of garlic. For a moment, I wonder why K is cooking spaghetti bolognaise so early in the morning. Then I fall back to sleep.

* * *

The kids. Their petty squabbles. The screams. My head feels like it's going to explode. I have to escape. Even for half an hour. K says he'll keep an eye on our three at the fun pool. Not that they need watching. They're all champion swimmers. You'd have to hold their heads under water for at least ten minutes to drown any of them. Though Sid, the teenager, would probably take longer.

I imagine my children's wide-eyed horror as I hold their heads under and jog out of the VR park, past the grand houses towards the woods, home to the old fun park and, perhaps, a slobbering wolf awaiting to serve up instant karma for my wicked thoughts. I turn into a field where a hairy, grey pony tugs at the long, juicy grass. It glances up, tossing its head at me and flattening its ears as if it's party to my ill imaginings. I push on, desperate for the cool of the woods. It's 10am but already mid-afternoon melting hot.

* * *

I wake again. Snatches of dreams of gruesome faces, mouths and chins protruding like muzzles, float around me and I think of Vincent van Gogh's *The Potato Eaters*, before the images fade. My head is rammed up against the headboard. There's something sharp digging into my skull. I'm too tired to investigate. I go back to sleep.

* * *

I crash into the woods like the shade's a finishing line for a race and stop to catch my breath. Something shiny up ahead catches my eye. It's a spade lying face down like it's had enough of the heat too, trying to bury itself into the cold earth. I wonder if there's been a recent digging class. Spade work is all the rage. Part of the manual labour movement. A two fingers up to the robos and drones. I wipe the sweat from my forehead, and follow the path, screams from the VR gamers bouncing off the trees. There's no getting away. K says it's a sacrifice we need to make for our kids to be kids. Only two more days and we're out of here.

* * *

My bed has sprouted more ridges and bumps, all digging into me and I know then I'm not where I should be. The seagulls begin squawking and light slowly oozes into the room. I tap my thumb. 5am. There's a message from my fixers.

'We've saved your life. We've dispersed a clot in your brain. Would you like to survey the damage?'

I nod.

'Under Premier FixYou™, you're not entitled to view images. Would you like to upgrade to Exclusive FixYou™ at a cost of $20,000?'

I give permission to access my credit card.

A few seconds later, a payment confirmation beeps, followed by before and after images of my skull. It's been caved in at the back but is now being axolotled.

'We strongly recommend statis until regrowth is complete. You are at 27 per cent regrowth. Pain blockers in place.'

I trawl through recent memories. Had I tripped and smashed my head against a tree trunk? Did K find me and take me to a statis centre?

* * *

I've come to see the old funfair rotting away. It gives me hope the VR park will one day go the same way. There's an intelligent barbed wire fence around it, its ugliness punctuated by even uglier KEEP OUT signs. I spot a small gap at the bottom where the sandy earth's been dug away, a clump of coarse yellow hair and its bloody roots stuck on several barbs. I turn my fixers onto silent, ready for the barbs to spin and slash at my hands and legs. I lift the wire and scoot under, sitting for a moment, watching the gashes on my arms and legs oozing blood before clotting. I stand and watch blood become powder, colouring the earth at my feet.

The old rollercoaster is up ahead. The undergrowth has partially hidden the tracks and, from a distance, it looks like the rusty carriages are flying through the branches. CampDutch spent millions reconditioning the rides for a retro park 70 years before. But its tame waterslides and rollercoasters could never compete with VR. So, after a year, they mothballed the lot.

Castle turrets rise through the bushes and on top of one is the park's mascot – a huge green frog. I find a long stick and smash my way through until I'm standing outside the castle. Yellow and pink roses steal up its plastic walls. I follow a path someone has beaten through the undergrowth and just as I'm wondering who it was, I find myself in a miniature village square. A twig snaps. I 360.

* * *

The Potato Eaters, one of Van Gogh's early paintings, depicts a family in a dark hovel tucking into potatoes. Everything about it is grim. The dullness of the colours, the poverty of furnishings, the fact they're eating potatoes and, the potato eaters themselves; goblin ugly. I mention this because I didn't think anyone looked like that any more. But I'm wrong because there's now one holding a shiny spade high above its head, about to smash it down on mine.

* * *

The shaft of light through the door widens then shrinks as a hooded figure approaches. It smells of garlic and unwashed bodies.

My fixers tell me my blood pressure is rocketing, and at the age of 67, I should cease doing whatever I'm doing before I lose my Exclusive cover. I close my eyes and breathe in and out, trying to block out the stench. I'd heard rumours. That they still lived in the last few forests of the world, breeding their disease-ridden, gene-defective children, despite the world wide ban. Every single Government had signed up to the Washington Treaty to cleanse their populations. Those who couldn't afford it, well, they naturally died out thanks to diabetes, heart disease, cancer and poor diet. It was kinder to end their suffering. Anyway, there were no jobs for them. A few had been kept in the Museum of Human Evolution. I'd even taken the kids to see them, paid for the overpriced cream tea experience, though the exhibits had refused to come out of the bedroom. The keepers had to use tasers to herd them into the garden but it made me feel uncomfortable, to be honest.

A toilet stench settles over me and my fixers start screaming again. The potato eater is shuffling towards me, wheezing and coughing and I can't help but panic about disease, even though I'm immune to everything. We learnt about disease at school. How illnesses like tuberculosis, cholera and typhus filled churchyards with tiny graves; how flu wiped out whole generations; genetic conditions atrophied your muscles until you were paralysed; or bad genes kept you addicted to alcohol and drugs. They're all long gone, I know. But.

'Asthma detected. No danger. Asthma is a breathing condition prevalent until 60 years ago,' say my fixers.

When I open my eyes, I see there's two potato eaters now. They're both short. 5ft 7ins at the most. I'd tower over them if I had a chance. I call up my MoodReader™. But itisn't working, or won't work because I realise the potato eaters won't have an equivalent. I have no idea what they want, but considering they've already caved my head in with a spade, I'm guessing it's not going to be good. I try and sit up but my arms and legs are bound.

One of the potato eaters leans over me, just as the other opens the door to let the light in. I catch its eyes. They're red, swollen, like someone has punched it in the face and when I glance away, I see I'm lying in a cot made of bones.

I pass out.

* * *

I wake to feel rough weather-worn hands on me and my fixer screaming into my ear.

'Several outdated communicable conditions: Athlete's Foot, herpes, warts, conjunctivitis, syphilis, chlamydia, chickenpox, measles, mumps. No danger.'

'Shut up,' I say.

The potato eaters step back.

'No, not you,' I say, taking in the bone cot.

Adult femurs mostly and a few pelvises. I wonder if they belong to those who died of disease. That it's some kind of primitive ritual, to keep the bones of your ancestors near to you.

They glance at one other and move closer. I see both have eye infections.

'I can get you medicine, food, anything you like. I'll pay, if you let me go. I won't tell anyone,' I say.

They ignore me. Their eyes are fixed on undoing the knots on my restraints.

'Do you understand? I can help you?' I repeat over and over, until it strikes me they must be deaf.

I remember learning about a movement among the Dutch hard of hearing community 45 years ago. They tried to set up their own colony, refusing to be cleansed. The Government rounded them up. Put them under house arrest until they died.

But had some managed to escape?

They sit me up. My arms are forced behind my back. My hands bound together with a piece of rough cloth. I try and struggle but I have no energy; my body is still in statis, programmed to put all its energy into regrowth just like the axolotl. They lift me out of the cot onto my feet and pull me towards the door. I duck to get through the tiny doorway and, as I blink in the bright sunlight, an explosion of yellows go off in my head. I steal a glimpse at my prison. It's one of the miniature town's shops; a bakery with a model dwarf kneading bread in the front window. Opposite is a sweet shop with seven dwarves sitting in the window, each poised to play a different musical instrument.

The potato eaters yank me across a bridge. I fall to my knees. They don't bother hauling me back up, but drag me into a courtyard. It's filled with dozens of rotting wooden benches, overlooking a stagnant, stinking pond. They lift me onto a bench at the front, sitting either side of me.

Facing us, on the opposite bank of the pond is a tumbledown shed and another potato eater, wearing a long hooded cloak made from an old pair of flowery orange curtains. It opens the shed doors to reveal a giant frog, sporting a sparkly blue tuxedo and a long curly green wig, perched over a keyboard. I want to laugh and take a photo for K and the kids, imagining us all giggling at the basic animatronics entertainment our ancestors used to enjoy. But the potato eaters are forcing me back up, dragging me to the edge of the pond.

And that's when I hear it. A soft grizzling at first, building into full blown cries. I think it must be a wild animal, until I see a bundle of rags lying at the frog's feet. A little foot kicks out, followed by an angry clenched fist. And I'm so focused on the poor baby, I don't notice I've been lifted up until I feel my feet sinking into the murky, brown water. When I hit the bottom, my feet slip on familiar knobbly bones, and I push up, breaking the surface, gulping in air. I spit out foul-tasting duck weed and glimpse the green-wigged frog staring at me, the little bundle at its feet now thrashing from side to side. I try to muster some strength and make a dive towards the bank nearby. But there is something holding me. One, two hands on my head. One, two hands on my shoulders, pinning me down, until my lungs are set to explode.

First published in the Future issue, Here Comes Everyone.

The Unravelling of Mr Growler

Mr Growler was a dog unlike any other during his trips to and from the harbour. It wasn't that he didn't enjoy all the usual canine pleasures like other less remarkable dogs. He enjoyed nothing better than chasing the skinny cats awaiting the arrival of the fishing boats, snuffling his way around the narrow, cobbled streets, the freshly gutted fish sending him into a sniffing frenzy. Nothing could distract him from the stench except a well placed kick from his owner, Mrs Emily Popkiss, a widow from the Dover Road.

No, it was his appearance that set him apart, often attracting squeals of delight from small children, and unkind and sometimes lewd remarks from the fishermen. It looked as though he was wearing an oversized and rather moth-eaten suit of thick brown fur. Emily was in no doubt that Mr Growler was fully aware of the effect he had on strangers. He often growled at passers-by who wandered too close and on occasions, objects, especially those that returned his own reflection. He even took offence against the waves that dared to wet his fat paws, snarling and biting at them as if their constant advance was a personal insult to his pride.

The pair made an odd couple. There was no real similarity between them as you sometimes see with certain dogs and their owners, except for both resembling pieces of furniture that Emily's late husband had lugged around Folkestone's West End. Emily resembled a well fashioned wardrobe, broad as wide, solid and dependable. On the other hand, Mr Growler was shaped like a tub of brandy similar to the ones smugglers sank and marked with a float until the coast was clear to bring them ashore.

Emily's husband had died of pneumonia two years before and she'd been left without any income. She had no other option than to fall back on her four brothers and the family business that she so detested. It wasn't that she didn't like her brothers. She loved them dearly. It was their trade she loathed for taking her father when she was just six years old.

However, her brothers were very persuasive. Mr Growler would make her a small fortune. A dog was an unlikely business partner, although her brother, John, had assured her that stranger vessels had been used: pig bladders full of French brandy secreted under the voluminous skirts of ladies; hollowed out loaves of bread containing delicate lace gloves; fishermen's boots stuffed with jewellery and petticoats lined with silk stockings. Even the dead lying in their coffins still had a purpose in life. They were sometimes gutted like the common cod and filled with lace, their heads, arms and hands remaining to fool any suspicious customs men.

Emily had found Mr Growler on the Warren one sunny May afternoon a year after her husband had died. She'd taken her nephew for a walk in the cliff top meadows, and had momentarily turned away to admire the swathes of aqua green sea when James vanished. She'd stumbled through the long grass shouting his name, fearing that the child had fallen over the cliff. Then she'd heard barking and frantically ran towards its direction and soon discovered James standing, white-faced and frozen still, next to a steep drop, while a bony, flea-infested dog circled him, baring his yellow fangs. As soon as Emily appeared, the creature had dropped to the ground and wagged its stumpy tail furiously.

The dog had followed them home and never left. His coat soon grew thick and shiny, although his temper never much improved. And while his little belly expanded in all directions, this was not strictly down to Emily's generous portions.

He had since earned a reputation as the Napoleon of the dog world, one that had been enhanced on their sixth return trip from Boulogne. A customs officer had made jest of his unruly fur and received a nip to his ankle. Emily had picked up Mr Growler and walked off without apology. Never again did any of customs officers bother them.

Emily followed Mr Growler as he waddled down the gangway from the steamship. The customs officers nodded respectfully as she and Mr Growler walked past and out into the harbour where a reddened sky met them. It would give them just enough light to walk to The Valiant Sailor where her brother was waiting, as always.

She'd avoided the pub for many years after her father had died. It wasn't the ruffians and the drunks who bothered her. It was the memory of her father's death. His friends had carried him from the Warren and wrapped his body in an old rug before laying him in front of the fire, as if the flames could lick some life back into him. Emily had knelt down beside him, while her mother and brothers unrolled the rug, recoiling at his bloated body. She'd touched his hand tentatively, feeling the cold, waxy skin of the dead and gently wiped the sand from his eyelids and from his blue lips. She then carefully peeled away the tiny strands of seaweed covering his handsome face and weather-beaten hands. These were the same hands that had given her such comfort and love. They now lay useless, battered and bruised by the waves that had drowned him. They were the same hands that had surprised her with gifts of chocolate, and sometimes, beautiful handmade Calais lace which London merchants fought over and smugglers died for.

And it was here, where her father had lain all those years ago, that the unravelling of Mr Growler would begin. Sensing it was an important and sombre occasion, Mr Growler stayed perfectly still on Emily's lap. First, she'd unpick the fine stitches, sown an hour before the steamship left for Boulogne, and peel off his hot, sweaty, and often foul-smelling rabbit fur suit. Then she'd slowly unfurl the fine lace from around his body, wrapping it around her left hand, until once again Mr Growler became just another dog.

The Unravelling of Mr Growler won the Folkestone Literary Festival's short story competition in 2009 and gave me the confidence to keep writing short stories. The dog has always stayed with me and a really nasty version appears in my children's book called The Stone of Surinam.

White Time

There's nowhere else to sit during second White Time, except opposite Bee Wee and her grunting sidekick, Wolf. So we reluctantly take up our seats, me squeezing Jarvis's hand a little bit harder than usual to warn him not to make eye contact.

The men place the White on the table in old chipped mugs of varying sizes. Some are decorated with pictures of animals, though I'm not sure of their names. I only remember rats, squirrats, mice and dogs, and they look nothing like them. Some have stupidly fluffy tails and fat paws. Others have rounded off shiny feet with no fur.

Quite a few of the mugs have chunky red writing on them telling us to 'K...E...E...P...C...A...L...M...A...N...D...C...A...R...R...Y...O...N,' which makes me laugh as I think, carry on with what exactly? Sleeping and drinking our endless mugs of White?

Today Jarvis has a mug I've never seen before.

'M...E...A...T...I...S,' I begin to spell out very slowly.

I'm the only kid who can read stuff, though I don't do it very well. The lessons with Grandma stopped after our wheelbarrow library turned to mulch.

I stop trying to work out the letters because Jarvis picks up the White, glugs it down, then slams the mug on the wooden table like he's in some kind of drinking White competition. He watches the White pool to the bottom then picks it up, his tongue darting out to reach the remaining drops.

'Look!' he says, peering inside.

At the bottom there's a picture of an animal with pointy shiny feet with a gap in the middle. It's tied upside down to a piece of wood hanging over a fire and doesn't look too happy about it either.

Black letters hover over the poor creature like flies.

'T...A...S...T...Y...T...A...S...T...Y...M...U...R...D...E...R.'

'What's *murder*?' asks Jarvis.

'When you kill someone,' I say.

'Kill someone?'

'Someone makes you die,' I say, pretending to drop dead onto the table.

I open my eyes and Jarvis is staring at me, his little face all screwed up in puzzlement. The wormy blue vein on his pale forehead is pumping with the effort of thinking.

I sit back up. 'You stop breathing. Your heart stops beating,' I say, thinking of Grandma.

'No way!'

'Yes way,' butts in a familiar voice.

I grab Jarvis' hand.

'We're all going to die at some point. But most of us are going to die sooner than others when we get sent up,' she says, looking up at the bumpy ceiling.

Wolf, raised by a pack of dogs, copies her but unlike Bee Wee his dopey blue eyes stay searching for something important up there in the chalk. After a few moments he gives up, and begins to yap as if he can smell an argument brewing.

'We don't know that,' I blurt out.

This time Jarvis squeezes my hand tightly because I've broken my own rule.

'We only know what they tell us,' I whisper.

'Oh, and you know different?' says Bee Wee, eyes narrowing and blinking rapidly like she's shooting out tiny daggers.

'That's what I'm saying; none of us know.'

'Where do you think everyone goes, stupid? You think we're going to live forever?' she says, pushing her ugly face across the table at us.

Wolf grunts. Jarvis nuzzles into me as Bee Wee bears down on him.

'Men in white going to train us up as soldiers so we can save the world. Don't you listen to anything, Jarvis, or are you as dumb as you look?'

'Don't call him dumb. He's only little.'

'I can call him what I like. I'm nearly there. Two more weigh ins and I'm 130lbs, then I'm out of here,' she says.

I fight the urge to punch her smug face. Last time, I was in isolation for two weeks. Jarvis missed me so much he refused to drink the White and was force fed through a tube.

'You should think yourself lucky the Lord saved you,' she says, crossing herself several times. 'We're the chosen ones. We were saved so we could save our country. Our Lord will reveal his plan for us when he's ready...'

I hug Jarvis, watching Bee Wee's White-coated moustache wriggling around like a deranged caterpillar as she sprouts all her God-bothering nonsense. She pauses every now and then to drink from her yellow mug. It's emblazoned with red writing.

'I'...D...A...G...R...E...E...W...I...T...H...Y...O...U...B...U...T... W...E'...D...B...O...T...H...B...E...W...R...O...N...G.'

I'm concentrating so hard on making the letters into words, and saying them out loud to myself, I don't see Bee Wee's mug coming towards me. A sharp pain rips across my forehead and there's wet blinding me. I think it's White until I see red spots decorating the table and a Jarvis-blur lurch across the table at Bee Wee, pulling her hair. The guards grab Jarvis and haul away a screaming Bee Wee while Wolf spins round in circles on all fours, howling.

* * *

The doctor is new. When she bathes the cut on my head, she looks me in the eye for a split second. And I can't draw mine away because hers are as blue as the sky I used to love gazing at. The skin around her eyes crinkles up like Grandma's and I wonder if she's smiling behind the mask.

I wince as three short bursts of ear drum splitting hell let us know the drones have stopped dropping their destruction. I swear it hurts more than the sound of the bombs, or my head being sliced open. Then comes the weekly announcement, repeated many times as if we're idiots: '*All occupants to the medical room, Tunnel 19 for weekly weigh in.*'

The doctor finishes messing with my head and hands me a pill and a glass of water. I swallow it and gag on its chalky flavour.

When she opens the door, Jarvis throws himself at me and we head down the corridor towards the entrance of Tunnel 19.

All the little ones are up first. There's always some new child refusing to stand on the weighing machine or keep in line. They can holler as much as they like but by the following week they're standing there all glazed eyes and quiet like the rest of us. Jarvis was the same. He was brought in not long after me, wailing his head off, stumbling around like a drunk as toddlers are apt to do. He'd throw himself on the floor, his face turning so purple I imagined him exploding, his limbs and body parts cheering the tunnel walls with vibrant shades of red. I'd stroke his sticky up blond hair and tickle him out of his rage, so the doctor could shove two mouthfuls of the hateful stuff into his mouth. Now he thinks I'm his mother.

Soon, it's my turn. I step onto the scales and watch the doctor writing down all the numbers flashing up on the screen. I see a smile in his eyes and look down at the scales. 125 pounds. I feel sick as I watch the doctor fetch the same red sweet Bee Wee boasted about eating. He holds it out to me. Jarvis is all wide green eyes. I bite the sweet in half, giving Jarvis the biggest bit. He slumps against the wall, eyes rolling back as the sugar hits. But I can't enjoy it because the sweet-giver is staring at me while talking to one of the guards. I reach for Jarvis's hand.

* * *

When the bombs get close, I calm myself by recalling Grandma's crazy tales of how families would get together for a Sunday dinner and eat animals; pig, chicken and beef and lamb and even a type of meat called veal where the animals were kept inside and fed only milk so their meat was pale. A real luxury, apparently.

'That world's long gone,' I can hear her saying. 'Trouble is they didn't stop burning the oil in time and the world boiled over, causing the floods and the deserts. And then they started messing with the animals, trying to clone them to adapt to less food. The perfect cow to give you the most milk and beef, the perfect pig for the juiciest pork chop. Cloned the life out of those poor animals.'

I never did get the chance to ask Grandma what cloning meant. I woke shivering in the night to find her frozen solid as the water tank. I snuggled up to her, willing her to snore her strange harmony of whistles and sporadic snorts to keep the ghost-wolves away. But she'd gone some other place without me. When the sun rose I noticed how she looked like a different person, someone younger, like the last 30 years of floods had never happened.

When the landowner found me, he had to prize my fingers from her stiff hands. Despite spitting, punching and kicking, just as Grandma taught me, he took me to Dover Tunnels. It's to protect you from war, he yelled above the sound of the bombs, stuffing a wad of dollars into his pocket as I was dragged into what I now know is a medical room, all shiny metal surfaces and a stink that made your eyes water. A doctor examined me and stuck a needle in my arm to draw blood, all the time bombarding me with questions about how I'd survived war.

'But Grandma told me the war finished just before I was born and now there's no food because of the floods.'

'You hear the bombs right now?' he asked as one exploded above us.

I put my hands over my ears and nodded.

'Well, then. Your grandma was wrong. There's plenty of war out there and you're lucky to be saved.'

I glanced at the chalk ceiling, wondering many things like why Grandma had lied, why we hadn't heard the bombs in the distance and how many bombs it'll take to destroy the beautiful castle I'd just seen on the hill.

'You ever see your grandma reading?' he asked.

My silence gave me away.

'What did she read?'

'I can't remember,' I said staring at my filthy feet.

'You know it's a criminal offence to read liespreaders.

'Can you remember what she read to you?'

'Murderous mermaids and stuff,' I mumbled.

The doctor looked at me properly for the first time.

'Half-woman, half-fish,' I explained. 'A gang of them went round killing fishermen. And then more weird stuff. There was a page called '*It happened to me.*''

The doctor raised an eyebrow. 'And what did happen?'

'Conspiracy theories, ghosts and alien abductions mostly.'

He made a funny snorting noise behind his mask. 'You remember what this magazine was called?'

'*Fortean Times*,' I said. 'Named after a man called Charles Fort. He wrote down all the strange things he saw.'

The doctor handed me a notebook and a stumpy pencil.

'Your grandma teach you to read and write?'

'Just my name.'

I was just starting on the second *E* when he snatched it away. 'You read well?'

I could see Grandma, shaking her head, finger on her lips, so I shook my head too.

* * *

I've not swallowed my White for 11 days. I've been keeping it in my mouth and spitting it out in the dark corners, or drinking just a little and knocking the rest over, blaming my clumsiness on the cut on my head. At first I was worried I was going to die because they said it contained anti this and anti that, words I didn't understand. But, in fact, I feel better than I've done for months. I'm beginning to feel more like I did when I lived with Grandma. More steady on my feet and more alert, so much so that I can smell the toilet stink of the tunnels. Far worse, though, is how clear the screams of the children trying to escape their nightmares are and the buzzing of the drones like giant mosquitos. I think how loud they must be up above and shudder.

Jarvis climbs into my bed as the drones and bombs get closer. He clamps himself so tightly to my chest that he feels like a second skin. It's an embrace I usually find comforting. But since I've stopped drinking the White, I want someone to make me feel safe.

I glance at the wall where I've been scratching important dates of events; my friends leaving, even Bee Wee and Wolf's departure a week ago. And something else too. I've started tracking the bombs. They come four times a week without fail - at night on days three and four, then during White Time three and ten on days five and seven. And that strikes me as stupid because they must be either terrible at aiming their bombs, or what they're trying to destroy is indestructible. But I wonder how that can be? I can carve into the chalk with a fingernail yet the bombs don't seem to scratch the surface of the tunnel network.

And another thought keeps me awake. I was safer in the countryside. There were no drones, bombs, men in white, but not much food. Yet in the midst of the bombing, we seem to have all the food we want. Fresh vegetables, rice, pulses, fish and endless cups of White. Bee Wee said it's to keep us strong for soldiering but I know now she's talking nonsense.

I can't keep still. I need to move. It's one of the side effects of not drinking White. Jarvis moans in his sleep as I try to unfurl him, so I carry him with me. The tunnel guard is slumped over a table, snoring. I look beyond him into the corridor which stretches out forever like the wide open jaws of a sea monster I'd seen once in *The Fortean Times*. I catch sight of the medical room at the end of the corridor, its metal door glinting at me like it's beckoning me over. And before I can stop myself, I'm standing in front of it. I pull down on the handle, expecting it to be locked but it opens easily and I walk into the dark room, blinking in the red light from the corridor behind me. Just a few feet away is the door that the doctors and guards come through. I shift Jarvis to my other shoulder and shuffle forward, my hand hovering over the handle before I push down. It clicks open and I poke my head around the door into another corridor, the walls stained with the familiar pale red light.

Right slopes downhill, left is up. I begin to climb, listening out for voices and footsteps. I hurry past several metal doors on either side and hear the familiar buzzing of the drone, so deafening it's like it's in the tunnel with us. I want to put my hands over my ears, over Jarvis' ears so he won't wake, but when I glance up at the tunnel ceiling, I spot the same black boxes where the commands blast out of. I stop in my tracks, staring up at them, trying to work out why they're broadcasting the sound of the bombs into the tunnels? It makes no sense, unless. Unless there are no bombs, just like there were no bombs when I lived with Grandma? My skin prickles at the thought and I push on. The passage ahead dips slightly and then turns to the right before rising steeply and stopping abruptly at the foot of a winding metal staircase.

I peer at the steps, wondering if I can really carry Jarvis all the way. Then I think of what I'd be leaving him to and a wave of claustrophobia pushes me up the stairs until a shaft of white light hits me and I lose my footing and stumble, falling into the rail, nearly dropping Jarvis. The light's so bright it has set off a series of orange and yellow explosions in my head. It was the same when the landowner snatched me, shining his torch into my eyes and I think the guards must have been waiting for us all along.

I wait for the guards to appear but after a few minutes, nothing happens so instead I wait for the colours to calm in my head and when I open my eyes and look up, I see blue above me and I understand. I climb the next four steps to the top, watching the dust and chalk dancing in the light, until I'm standing at the top of the stairs, the corridor ending in a bright blue door of sky. I peak out into the blue, blinking back the light for several moments until my eyes tell me the tunnel has come out on a road which drops sharply down a hillside covered in grass so green it looks like it's showing off. Beyond is more blue, its waves crashing into white cliffs and...

I have to blink several times because I think my eyes are playing tricks on me. And when I peer out again, I feel the ground shifting beneath my feet. Because I can see thousands of houses dotted along the coast with not a chimney stack out of place. Huge ships too are docking and I swear there are even cars moving on the streets. I shut my eyes, again, thinking the light is playing tricks. But when I open them, the houses, the ships, the cars are still there, glistening in the sun. I check no one is around and poke my head out, at least expecting to see a huge pile of stone where the castle stood. But, instead, it's standing proud at the top of the hill, the red crusader flag flapping in the wind, exactly as it was when I was brought here all those years ago.

I want to wake Jarvis. Tell him there is no stupid war. But another thought comes. Another thought I don't want to acknowledge: why keep us in the tunnels if there is no war? I push the thought away as a low growling rolls down the hill from the castle. I slink back into the tunnel, glimpsing a flash of metal speeding past. I wait for a few moments and stick my head out. A lorry has stopped at a red barrier. It has fancy black lettering on the side. I catch an L...U...X before I get distracted by the driver jumping out to greet a guard in white. They shake hands before ambling round to the back. The driver opens the doors and the guard looks in, turning his head to the side as if whatever's inside isn't the right way up. I don't catch what he says but the driver throws his head back as if he's heard the funniest thing in the world. I focus on the words on the lorry, desperately trying to work out what the curls, curves and licks mean. But the lights in my head make them jump around and I can't catch their meaning. I give up and watch the men disappear inside a small brick building.

I check no one is coming, and run to the lorry. I yank the lever I saw the driver pull and the door swings open. Icy air hits me, followed by a vile stench like the tunnel toilets. I slide Jarvis along the floor, climb up and close the doors behind me, knocking into several heavy objects hanging from the roof. I start to shiver and hug Jarvis to me, wondering how long we'll survive in our thin cotton suits, and whether I'd made a stupid mistake. That we should get out. Like, right now.

But it's too late. The engine roars to life and we're heading down the hill. We round a sharp bend and one of the doors swings open before slamming shut and I think I catch sight of solid blood red and bone white objects hanging from hooks. I'm just thinking how similar they are to the rats me and Grandma used to skin when we turn sharply, and the other door crashes open. Light floods in, illuminating dozens of waxy pink creatures trussed up by their feet and I sink to the floor as I recognise Bee Wee's beady eyes staring at me and next to her, Wolf bearing his raggedy yellow teeth for the very last time. And I feel something ooze down my spine as Grandma's tale about the baby cows kept inside suddenly comes back to me at the same time as the words on the side of the lorry finally make sense.

Tiger Talking

My neighbour, Louise, was the first to spot the tigers during lockdown.

'Outside the old sea captain's house. The house opposite yours. I'm not joking. I'm really not,' she told me over the phone in her customary style of repeating everything twice; something that'd grown into a habit after having to apologise for her three bitey dogs, all now muzzled.

I yanked open the bedroom curtains and sucked in my breath. Sure enough there was the tiger and its cub now standing at the bus stop as if waiting for a ride into town to do some tiger shopping, whatever that may be.

'No shopping bags. No evidence of any shopping bags stored in tiger pockets', said Louise as if picking up on my thoughts. 'You better call that Mayor friend of yours. Call her now. She'll have the number. Mr Tiger Talker. The tiger talking man,' she added.

I hung up and rang Carol straightaway.

'I'll call him now,' said Carol. 'But whatever you do, don't let them tigers out of your sight.'

I did as she asked, watching their every move. Both were sniffing at something on the pavement before turning their attention to the old sea captain's prize-winning roses. I was just fretting whether or not to call the bus company to warn the driver not to let them on, when Carol rang back.

'It's no good,' she said. 'We're a week too late. Poor Slacker died of the coronavirus.'

I watched the cub playfully jumping up at his mother and shivered as she batted him away with a giant paw, thinking of what went before our golden tiger-free years.

'He's the last in the line of the tiger talkers,' continued Carol. 'I should have listened to him at last year's meeting.'

I was there. I remember Slacker pleading for the community to offer up an apprentice. But everyone found something more interesting to look at on their phones. Tiger talking was as uncool among teenagers as it was too us middle agers. There was even talk of enforced tiger talking lessons at school but parents refused, believing it to be mumbo jumbo. The general consensus was there was no need because no one had seen a tiger in town for 15 years.

'Everyone's just going to have to watch their backs,' said Carol.

* * *

It was my grandma's 90th birthday. It'd been five weeks since lockdown and six weeks since she'd reluctantly moved into the care home. Although there was a strict ban on visitors, the care home manager said she'd arrange for Grandma to appear on the balcony like the Queen, so I could wish her happy birthday. And although both mother and cub had scarpered back towards the forest, thanks to a blast of the old sea captain's fog horn, I still sprinted to my car and locked myself in.

However, all thoughts of tigers flew out of the window when I saw Grandma standing on the balcony. Her lank grey hair, usually flecked with talcum powder, had been dyed platinum blonde and curled in the style of a 1940s starlet. Gone were her grubby grey trackie bottoms and favourite pink hoodie she refused to take off, even at night, despite the array of stains decorating it. Instead, she wore a pretty bluebell print tea dress.

'You like?' she asked, pushing up the curls several times as if her very persistence could defy the laws of gravity.

'You look 20 years younger,' I told her.

'Frank says 25,' she replied, before turning to shut the balcony doors and putting a long plum-coloured nail to her remarkably plump lips. 'Shh. I've told him I'm only 82! He's just turned 85.'

'A toy boy, Grandma?'

She cocked her head to the side and smiled impishly, fluttering long fake eyelashes before taking out her little mirror from her bag and pouting into it.

'Are you actually my grandma?' I asked, gawping at this animated version of the frail lady I'd reluctantly said goodbye to weeks before.

She stopped admiring herself in her mirror and looked down at me sharply.

'I'm just saying it's unusual for someone to go into a care home looking like a bag lady and coming out looking like a film star,' I explained.

'You think so?' she said, checking herself in the mirror again. 'I suppose I do look alright. Janine, my best friend in here, used to be a beautician. She's got the lot; fillers, botox and this electric pulse machine that lifts everything up.'

'Including your legs? Where's your walker?' I asked.

'Frank said to ditch the Ws; walkers and wheelchairs are for losers. I need support, not care. Got me walking up and down the garden every day and doing squats to strengthen my butt. Told me I'd become too dependent on people like you.'

I felt myself bristle at being dismissed as 'people like you' after being her carer for two years. But I didn't have long to wallow because she spun round and slapped her shapely behind.

'Grandma!' I gasped, glancing around the deserted street. 'Well, at least I won't have to listen to you scream every time you see a kerb or a hairline crack in the pavement,' I added.

'It was a trust issue, that's all,' she said. 'Imagine having a child wheeling you around.'

'I'm nearly forty -,' I protested.

'I don't care how old you are. It's what was in here', she said, stabbing a manicured nail at her head. 'It didn't feel safe.'

'But cosmetic surgery is? I mean, does this Janine have a licence?'

'Oh, listen to you Mrs Squaro.'

'Mrs Squaro? Me?' I muttered, wondering what type of people she was hanging around with, and who the hell this Frank was who had so much influence over her.

'Who cares if Janine does, or doesn't have a licence. We're all at risk of dying from the plague if you hadn't noticed,' she said.

'And now being eaten by a tiger,' I replied, telling her all about the two at the bus stop.

'I'll talk to Frank,' she said, suddenly all serious. 'He was Slacker's best friend. Used to go down to the forest with him at weekends. By all accounts, he picked up quite a bit of tiger talking.'

And with that she was gone. I hadn't even wished her a 'happy birthday'.

* * *

I needn't have worried. The following day, I get a call from the care home manager asking me to come over for a balcony chat. I thought maybe grandma had overdosed on Janine's fillers, or her and this Frank had absconded. But when I arrived, Grandma was waiting at the entrance. Holding her hand was a strikingly handsome man. He was dressed in a tailored grey suit lined with bubblegum pink satin, a matching pink shirt and garish orange tie, all topped off with a trilby hat he tipped at me as I got out of the car.

The manager waved from the balcony, telling me it had all been arranged with the Mayor. Frank was our only hope in keeping the tigers out, she said. She threw down gloves and a mask and told me I needed to drop Frank off at the edge of the forest. Once there, we were to stay in the car while Frank did his tiger talking.

When I turned to go, Grandma and Frank were already snuggled up in the back seat of the car. I climbed into the driver's seat and Frank leant towards me, proffering his elbow.

'Iris has told me so much about you,' he said, before he and Grandma started giggling about something or other.

It was only a few minutes' drive to the forest. Nonetheless, I had problems keeping my eyes on the road with all their carrying on in the back. I was relieved to catch sight of the bridge to the forest and beaches up ahead and, in the distance, the two great memorial arches spanning both ends. The first arch commemorated the 334 townsfolk who'd died trying to hunt, capture or tame the tigers before the Tiger Pact of 1988. The second paid tribute to the five tigers slain since The Great Tigerinho's Circus was shipwrecked on our shores 300 years ago.

'Have you actually done this before, Frank?' I asked, noticing both had stopped fooling around as we passed through the first arch.

'No, but if I don't do something then the tigers will never leave the town alone,' he replied.

'Remember that French teacher? Mrs Dadler?' I asked.

I saw Frank wince and immediately felt mean for mentioning her.

'She always thought she was better than everyone else that woman but the tigers certainly taught her a lesson,' he said. 'She forgot the one thing that keeps them tigers out of town. Aretha Franklin knew it and so do many decent folk.'

I went to say that Aretha had actually been talking about men, not tigers, but let the words fall silent.

'We don't encroach on their land and they don't encroach on ours. That's the law of the town. Mrs Dadler got greedy, that's all,' Frank said.

'But, aren't you worried about - ?'

'Being eaten?' interrupted Frank. 'I'm nearly 92.'

'You told me you were 85,' said Grandma, the wrinkles on her forehead struggling to furrow against her frozen muscles.

'And you, my dear, told me you were 82,' replied Frank, squeezing her knee. 'I can think of no nobler death than being eaten by a tiger. Anyway, it shouldn't come to that. A lot of Bob's tiger talking has come back to me since I retired.'

We were close to the forest now, and in the mirror, I glimpsed tears rolling down Grandma's cheeks before she threw herself upon Frank.

'Please don't go. I've only just found you. You're the only man I've ever loved!' she pleaded.

'What about Grandpa?' I said.

She ignored me, clinging onto Frank as I parked next to the no-man's land, a two-acre zone where in normal circumstances no human, nor tiger could pass.

'It's all going to be tickety-boo,' said Frank, untangling Grandma from him before striding towards a clearing at the entrance to the tigers' territory where the black and orange stripy army were gathering.

Grandma grabbed my gloved hand as we watched Frank arrive at the gate where the tigers began to line up in neat rows. She squeezed my hand tightly as a huge tiger, its skin stretched and hanging down its flanks in great folds, broke from the formation and strolled towards Frank. Frank tipped his hat as he was wont to do and the tiger rose up on two legs, resting its paws on the gate as if they were two neighbours having a chat about the weather over a garden fence. Frank gesticulated to the town and to the forest, all the time the tiger following his movements with his bright amber eyes and letting out a series of soft understanding growls.

After a few minutes, Frank shrugged as if to say 'that's all I got, my friend' and, with that, the head honcho tiger jumped down from the gate. He strode back to his army which turned and slid into the forest, momentarily lighting up the forest with flashes of golden stripes, until the forest was once again a solid green.

Frank turned too and ambled back to the car, stopping at a patch of wild purple poppies, gesturing for Grandma to turn away while he picked a fulsome bunch.

'There you go,' he said, passing them over to Grandma. 'From one beautiful flower to another.'

I rolled my eyes and turned on the engine.

'Well,' I said, 'what did the tigers have to say for themselves?'

'They apologised profusely,' said Frank, wiping away Grandma's tears with a starched orange hankie. 'But because it was so quiet and - what with the weather being so nice and with no one on the beaches - they thought we'd all left. Or been abducted by aliens,' added Frank.

'Aliens?' I said as we exited no-man's land.

'That's tigers for you,' shrugged Frank.

I wrote this story for my mother, Ida, who was ill in hospital in 2020 and read it to her in the week she died. I miss you, Mum.

Homecoming Queen & Other Twisted Tales is Michele's first short story collection and was published in paperback in 2021. The title comes from her story set on Folkestone Harbour Arm, Kent, England. If you ever visit, have a look out for the QR code to listen to a recording of the story.

She is also the author of the *Missing Fur* series, wildlife conservation-themed books for children aged from 8-12. *The Mystery of the Missing Fur* is the first in the series and follows Bernard's adventures after he saves three rare Amazonian monkeys and a zoo full of animals from the clutches of a vain celebrity, a short-sighted trophy hunter and a grinder of endangered animal bones, tusks and horns.

The second in the series, *The Macaw of Doom*, sees a mysterious stranger turning up at Bernard's door claiming to be his long-lost cousin and touches on the illegal trade in exotic birds.

Her first children's book, *The Stone of Surinam*, is a time travel adventure set just after the Great Fire of London and involves three amazing children, wheelie shoes, kidnapping, a mean dog and an even meaner dog owner.

If you want to find out more about Michele's other writing, please visit her website at www.michelesheldon.com and sign up to her newsletter on Substack.

www.ingramcontent.com/pod-product-compliance
Lightning Source LLC
Chambersburg PA
CBHW021248200726

48288CB00015B/2755